STAMPEDE!

To Slocum's left was a high point that he figured would be avoided by the stampede. The climb was tough, but he reached the top in time to see the wide front of charging cattle like a dark mat coming down the valley. Riders on both sides were shooting their guns in the air to hurry them onward. He drew the shotgun to his shoulder and began firing at any form. A rider went down. Another's mount struck by the shot went bucking into the night. They returned some pistol fire, but by then he was on his belly sending buckshot at any red flashes of pistol shots.

The herd never stopped. The stretched barb wire screamed and then popped under the charge of the wide front. He knew, laying belly down on the rocks and sharp thorns, that their still-thundering hooves were shredding and trampling Myra's hay crop to nothing.

Damn you, Grant! Slocum was sprawled on the ground, his face in the alkali-tasting dust. If only he'd acted faster. Grant had rounded up a whole herd of old, toothless longhorn steers—not worth a dollar for their hides even—and stampeded them through her place. Shredding the whole crop. *Damn, you want war, you are going to get it . . .*

DON'T MISS THESE
ALL-ACTION WESTERN SERIES
FROM THE BERKLEY PUBLISHING GROUP

THE GUNSMITH by J. R. Roberts

Clint Adams was a legend among lawmen, outlaws, and ladies. They called him . . . the Gunsmith.

LONGARM by Tabor Evans

The popular long-running series about Deputy U.S. Marshal Long—his life, his loves, his fight for justice.

SLOCUM by Jake Logan

Today's longest-running action Western. John Slocum rides a deadly trail of hot blood and cold steel.

BUSHWHACKERS by B. J. Lanagan

An action-packed series by the creators of Longarm! The rousing adventures of the most brutal gang of cutthroats ever assembled—Quantrill's Raiders.

DIAMONDBACK by Guy Brewer

Dex Yancey is Diamondback, a Southern gentleman turned con man when his brother cheats him out of the family fortune. Ladies love him. Gamblers hate him. But nobody pulls one over on Dex . . .

WILDGUN by Jack Hanson

The blazing adventures of mountain man Will Barlow—from the creators of Longarm!

TEXAS TRACKER by Tom Calhoun

Meet J.T. Law: the most relentless—and dangerous—man-hunter in all Texas. Where sheriffs and posses fail, he's the best man to bring in the most vicious outlaws—for a price.

JAKE LOGAN

SLOCUM AND THE SULFUR VALLEY WIDOWS

J

JOVE BOOKS, NEW YORK

THE BERKLEY PUBLISHING GROUP
Published by the Penguin Group
Penguin Group (USA) Inc.
375 Hudson Street, New York, New York 10014, USA
Penguin Group (Canada), 90 Eglinton Avenue East, Suite 700, Toronto, Ontario M4P 2Y3, Canada
(a division of Pearson Penguin Canada Inc.)
Penguin Books Ltd., 80 Strand, London WC2R 0RL, England
Penguin Group Ireland, 25 St. Stephen's Green, Dublin 2, Ireland (a division of Penguin Books Ltd.)
Penguin Group (Australia), 250 Camberwell Road, Camberwell, Victoria 3124, Australia
(a division of Pearson Australia Group Pty. Ltd.)
Penguin Books India Pvt. Ltd., 11 Community Centre, Panchsheel Park, New Delhi—110 017, India
Penguin Group (NZ), Cnr. Airborne and Rosedale Roads, Albany, Auckland 1310, New Zealand
(a division of Pearson New Zealand Ltd.)
Penguin Books (South Africa) (Pty.) Ltd., 24 Sturdee Avenue, Rosebank, Johannesburg 2196,
South Africa

Penguin Books Ltd., Registered Offices: 80 Strand, London WC2R 0RL, England

This is a work of fiction. Names, characters, places, and incidents either are the product of the author's imagination or are used fictitiously, and any resemblance to actual persons, living or dead, business establishments, events, or locales is entirely coincidental.

SLOCUM AND THE SULFUR VALLEY WIDOWS

A Jove Book / published by arrangement with the author

PRINTING HISTORY
Jove edition / October 2005

Copyright © 2005 by The Berkley Publishing Group.

ISBN: 0-515-14018-X

JOVE®
Jove Books are published by The Berkley Publishing Group,
a division of Penguin Group (USA) Inc.,
375 Hudson Street, New York, New York 10014.
JOVE is a registered trademark of Penguin Group (USA) Inc.
The "J" design is a trademark belonging to Penguin Group (USA) Inc.

PRINTED IN THE UNITED STATES OF AMERICA

10 9 8 7 6 5 4 3 2 1

Prologue

Hot wind picked up small puffs of dust off the caliche ground. Standing on the porch with his gloved hand resting on the smooth porch post, he squinted against the glaring sun. His stare directed to the south across the sea of dull green greasewood bushes for sight of the stage. He shifted his weight to both of his boot heels and drew out the gold watch from his leather vest: two fifteen. The stage was thirty minutes late.

"Gawdamnit, Jericho, where's he at?"

"I can't say rightly," the completely bald-headed station keeper said, coming out under the palm frond-topped porch to join him. Jericho's voice had a reedy, nasal sound and he walked half stooped over by the arthritis in his spine.

"Who's driving today?"

"Billy Marrow. Best man they've got."

"Looks like anyone could get a stagecoach over that country out there to here on time."

"Well, there's breakdowns and"—Jericho went to using his fingers to count off the excuses—"Mechanical, broken axle, a mule down, and there could be Injun trouble. Lord, who knows?"

"One thing for certain, you don't." The man shook his head with impatient disapproval.

"Who you come for, anyway?"

"The boss's daughter. She's coming in from boarding school back east."

Jericho straightened some and used his hands for shade to look southward.

"Word's out that them Apaches ain't happy over there at San Carlos."

1

"Your squaw say anything about it?"

Jericho shook his head. "Naw, she don't talk about them. I heard that from a buck came by here the other day."

"Hell, I wouldn't like San Carlos either. But they can go up in the White Mountains."

"That ain't their own land."

"No, they want the Chiricahua and Dragoon Mountains back. I savvy that." He could see the far-off purple range south of them.

"They can bitch all they want. They'll never give it back to them." Jericho started to go inside when the air buzzed with the swish of arrows. Three struck the station man in the back and made him stand upright as a strangling "ah" escaped his lips. He fell facedown in the doorway.

Philip Manley's hand went for his gun butt in his holster. Too late. Three more arrows tipped with razor sharp steel points thudded into his chest, and he sank to his knees. Then numb-like he slumped to his butt with his back to the post. Like the drip from a water barrel he felt his life slipping away. The clatter of horses arriving and the coyote yipping of the angry warrior-riders came next. A shadow passed into his vision, and he saw Jericho's young wife, Chee, come out the door carrying a small bundle.

She bent over and unbuckled her man's gun belt, then ripped it off him. A small smile in the corners of her dark lips, she spat in his face and said something guttural at him.

With the buckle relatched, she slung the six-gun holster over her shoulder with a small sack under her arm, and went to join the buck talking to her from horseback.

In a flash of her brown legs, she bounded up behind him and hugged his waist tight. No doubt—they knew each other. Then the half dozen bucks with him raised their bows and rifles and began to scream in Apache about their success.

In his fading eyesight, Manley saw her. A white girl of perhaps seventeen–eighteen, with her long blond hair glinting like gold in the sunshine—the expensive blue dress torn, and her white petticoats showing—sitting astride a milling paint horse clinging for her life to its mane, being led away by an angry-faced Apache buck. Amantha Grant—Chiricuha captive.

His boss, Albert Grant, would be pissed. Manley's head

slumped forward, and a great cloud of darkness began to shade out his vision. Like a knife, his breath came harder each time. Precious blood was being pumped out with every beat of his heart until it too wound down.

1

Thick tobacco smoke filled the room with a yellow haze from the candle lamps. Over in the corner, some TB-afflicted guy was bent forward in a chair, and for the last thirty minutes had tried to cough his lungs up. A drunk doxy named Soapy sat on the bar with her dress and slips wadded up to her waist. Her skinny legs spread apart, she was showing some half-drunk old man her merchandise. Freddie's Oracle Saloon in Beggar's Wash, Arizona Territory, was also the site of a serious poker game.

The man holding three aces and two queens—John Slocum—was slouched down in the captain's chair considering his opponents' possibilities. After four hours of serious gambling, he was over a hundred dollars ahead. The jackpot in the center of the table represented over two hundred dollars more.

Pecos Bob Stone was out. Ramsey Carter looked ready to toss in his cards. The center of attention was a pale-faced man, his features harsh under the drawn skin. He eyed the pot and then his hand several times, clicked together a couple ten-dollar gold pieces like he aimed to raise, then in the end he called.

"Full house," Slocum said. "Aces over queens."

Ramsey grinned, shook his head, and then tossed in his cards. "Got me beat."

Tuff Coburn laughed. "Damn, I knew it was good, but never dreamed that good. I had a house with jacks and fives."

Slocum looked at the gaunt fellow across from him. "Well, Doc?"

The blue eyes twinkled. The thin lips under the trimmed mustache never moved. Then he nodded and tossed his cards in. "I had three aces too." Then he laughed at his own joke until he

4

joined his fellow lunger in uncontrollable coughing. "But gawdamn—I knew one of you could count higher than four!"

Slocum gathered in all the money, stood, and swept it off into his hat. "My pleasure gents. Been a fun afternoon."

"How shall I ever recover my losses?" Doc asked.

"Playing some other sucker," Slocum said and nodded to the circle. "Been nice guys. I hate to leave with your money, but better than the reverse."

"Absolutely," Doc Holliday said. "Come to Tombstone sometime. We have grand cockfights every Sunday."

"That fucking Earp still there?" Pecos Bob asked.

"Do you mean Wyatt, sir?"

"You know who I mean."

"Where did you get that sour impression of my good friend?"

"That sum bitch coldcocked me in a bar in Dodge. Minding my own business mind you."

"Did he apologize?"

"Yeah, sort of later, but he still pissed me off."

"Hell, Bob, lots of things piss you off," Ramsey said and shook his head to dismiss any concern, then began to deal. "Every one ante in five bucks. See yeah, Slocum."

"How much did you win sweetheart?" A house-girl called Lilly took his arm and steered him to the bar.

She began to stack the coins up in small piles on the bar. Slocum counted the folding money and jammed all hundred thirty-two dollars in his front pocket. Then he began counting her stacks. Two-hundred eighty in small coins, thirty of it in five-dollar whorehouse tokens. Made over four hundred dollars. Not a bad evening's wages. He waved Scully, the barkeep, over.

"Bring the lady and I some good whiskey."

"Coming right up."

She moved in close, bumped her hip to his, and smiled big. "You want an all-nighter or just a toss?"

"They say you're the wildest thing in these parts." He rested his elbow on the bar to consider the deep cleavage showing in the low-cut front of her dress.

She laughed. "I heard you'd make a mare squeal with your prod."

"All lies." He looked up as a man busted through the front doors.

"I'm looking for a guy named Slocum. He in here?"

Slocum twisted and used his arm to keep Lilly out of the way.

"What do you need from him?" Slocum asked, wiping his palm on the side of his leg in case he needed his gun hand for action.

"My boss wants to see him pronto?"

"Who's you boss?"

"Albert Grant."

Slocum considered the out-of-breath drover standing on the platform before you stepped down two flights of steps into the saloon. Albert Grant could go straight to hell for all he cared about the big cattleman that had recently moved into the Sulfur Springs Valley. Grant could take all his Texas gunslingers, wad them up, and go back to the Lone Star State for all he cared about him after running roughshod on some nice Mormon "widows." Several of those women lost their husbands when the law on polygamy went into force. Slocum had been dropping by and helping several of them. Especially Myra Downing. Only a week before, he'd bucked down a couple of Grant's men at her place and sent them packing.

"Mister, Grant's offering you a thousand dollars to come see him."

"I ain't for sale." Slocum turned back to the bar and raised his glass to Lilly like the man did not exist.

"That's lots of money," she said and then made a raised eyebrow as if to say *What the hell.*

"All you've got to do is ride down and talk to him."

Slocum looked at himself in the mirror behind the bar. Clean-shaven for once. New gray vest, nice blowzy sleeved white shirt with red garters on the sleeves, gray silk kerchief to match the vest, and a pair of striped black wool pants. Soft goatskin boots that molded his feet, and even his black felt hat looked clean—why would he want to flour it with all that dust riding down to the Grant Headquarters.

"Slocum—my final offer. Fifteen hundred."

"Shit!" Lilly swore. "For that much money, Honey, I'd carry you piggyback down there."

The whiskey to his lips, he set it down and looked hard at the young man. "What in the hell does he want me to do?"

"You hear about them renegades broke out San Carlos?"

"Cherry cows?"

"Yeah, some sub chief named Wolf and five bucks."

"They're probably deep in the Sierra Madres right now."

"They struck the Fort Grant stage near the Meer Creek Station, yesterday. Took Grant's daughter Amantha hostage, then killed his ranch foreman Philip Manley and also pin-cushioned old Jericho who ran the station."

"I thought Jericho had a young Apache wife?" Slocum asked.

"She ain't nowhere around. Either left with them or they took her too."

Slocum tossed down half the whiskey left in his glass and let it run like hot lava down his throat. That meant they'd killed the driver and guard, too.

"Billy Marrow and Sledge dead?" he asked.

"Yeah, they cooked Billy's brains out over a fire. Him spread-eagle upside down on a wheel." Then Grant's hand made a sickening face.

"Didn't Manley wear them leather cuffs and consider himself a gun hand?"

"Yeah, but he never got a chance to fire a shot. Had three arrows in the middle of his chest. Any one of them would have killed him."

"And Jericho?"

"Someone noticed they took his gun and holster. He was shot in the back with arrows and whoever took his gun set broke off the shafts flipping him over. But they never bothered taking Manley's gun."

"Anything else missing?"

"Yeah, folks said old Jericho had some money. Several hundred dollars, maybe even more. His money box was gone. And while most squaws don't have many things, none of her stuff was there."

"What's Grant want out of me?" Slocum studied Lilly's shape in the mirror back of the bar. Why did this Grant deal keep niggling him? He could image Lilly's ripe figure in bed—naked as Eve. Probably buck wilder than a mink bitch. His vital parts itched for her swollen walls to scratch him.

"He wants his daughter Amantha back."

"Where's Tom Horn?" Slocum asked, dropping his elbows on the bar and nodding at the bartender that he wanted a refill, the same for her.

"Working for Pinkerton. Colorado, they say."

"Chief of scouts. Al Sieber?"

"Down in Mexico working a gold mine."

"How in the hell did you find me?"

The cowboy looked around and finally shrugged. "I asked Myra Downing."

Slocum nodded, paid the bartender off the stack of coins on the bar for the fresh drinks. "What's your name?"

"Roy Gene Hartford."

"Roy Gene, huh?"

"Yes, sir."

"You Grant's new foreman?"

"No, sir."

"Then how come he sent you?"

"Well, Manley was killed and he ain't found a new foreman—yet."

"I ain't got much use for your boss. Number two, going down in the Madras looking for a white Apache hostage is like looking for a fleck of gold in a barrel of flour."

"Mister, if you ever saw a picture of her, you'd—well, be plumb upset that anyone that pretty was being raped and beat by them gawdamn savages."

Slocum nodded, ready for another shot of whiskey. "Third, she's probably dead by now. Takes a tough one to live under their conditions."

"Would you come to the ranch and at least talk to Mr. Grant?"

Slocum clinked his glass against Lilly's. "Here's looking at you, darling. All I'm going to get to do today." They both downed their shots. Then he shoved twenty dollars in coins to her. "But I expect a two-day stand for this when I get back."

She threw her arms around him and began kissing his face. "For that big man, you can have three."

"I have to go get my horse," Slocum said to the barkeep, pushing the rest of the coin money over. "Put all this in the safe. I don't come back in three months, you give it to her."

"Oh, darling, you're coming back," she said, hanging onto his arm as they headed for the door.

"Slocum," Roy Gene said. "I already picked up your horse at the livery and paid the outstanding bill against him. He's right out there."

That boy thought of everything. Slocum parted the batwing doors and there stood his red roan horse, Strawberry, a tough bulldog mountain horse hitched to the rack and standing undisturbed in the midafternoon hot sun. He nodded and turned back to Lilly, took her in his arms, and kissed her hard on the mouth, while she openly ran her hand over the rise in his pants.

"Hate to see you leave like that," she said, sounding concerned and then grinned big, stepping back from him.

"That's the way things are. Right, Roy Gene?" Slocum undid the reins.

"I guess," the cowboy said, getting in his own saddle.

Slocum could have sworn the boy was blushing. He shook his head and headed Strawberry after him. This could only be a fool's mission—the only thing Slocum couldn't figure out was who was the biggest, him or Grant. The two men short loped southward.

2

Grant's headquarters and mansion were still under construction. A mile beyond the new Southern Pacific tracks and in sight of the Chiricuhuas, the sprawling corrals and fresh leveled fields spread out for some distance down the Sulfur Valley. To the west were the strange shallow lakes that looked almost like oceans in this arid land. A hundred fifty feet underneath the surface was a strong water system—artesian—all one had to do was poke a hole in the ground and water came out in a gusher. Down the valley, several Mormon "widows" farmed. They, too, tapped the underground source to irrigate their alfalfa and Mexican corn crops. Their small tillable plots of forty to eighty acres had drawn the wrath of this newcomer who wanted the entire country to himself.

When Slocum dropped out of the saddle, a young Mexican boy rushed out to take their horses. He hitched his pants, looked around at the two-story mansion, the freshly planted palm trees, and all the activity.

A squat-built man came out on the porch. His face square like some mastiff's, he smoked a cigar, wore a black silk robe, and had the airs about him of someone who considered himself damn important. Slocum nodded to him and followed Roy Gene.

"Mr. Grant, this is Slocum," the young cowboy said, out of breath.

"Good day, Slocum," Grant said. He never offered to shake hands. "Come inside and have a drink. We can talk better in there."

Slocum followed the two of them inside; the tough-sounding Grant and the anxious Roy Gene. They went through a foyer with glazed Mexican tile and into a great two-story room where Grant led them to a bar. The room was in the process of being plastered by several Mexican workers.

"Whiskey's fine with you, Slocum?" Grant asked.

"Fine." He craned his head around to see the sheet draped over the painting high on the wall. If it was a person, it must be life size. Strange, it was covered, while the Arabian city scene wasn't concealed, nor the three French countryside ones Slocum suspected were both by masters.

"I collect art," Grant said, handing him a glass.

"I see. Some museum pieces, no doubt. The covered one?"

"A painting done by the artist Molay. It is of my daughter Amantha, God bless her. The one whom the Apaches took hostage."

"I see."

"No, you don't. My wife died a year ago. Amantha is all I have."

"You know that her chances of being alive are very small."

"I have reliable reports that she was still alive when those savages rode into the Sierra Madres."

"For enough money, I'd tell you she was alive, too." Slocum found another painting on the wall. This one of a plumb nude on a fainting couch.

"You don't believe the reports?" Grant asked.

"Not without seeing her myself."

"I believe them. I believe them enough I want to hire you. They say you are the best around to track down Apaches in Mexico."

"After Tom Horn and Al Sieber. And some others." Slocum held out his glass and Grant splashed more whiskey in it.

"She looks like a bed full, Roy Gene." Slocum gave a head toss toward the nude.

The up-until-then quiet cowboy swallowed hard and then managed a strangled, "Yeah, she does."

"How much do you want to go look for her?" Grant asked, ignoring Slocum's teasing of his hand.

"Conditions, first," Slocum said, resting his elbows on the bar and looking at the huge table and chairs that would easily seat twenty.

"What are they?"

"There are a half dozen Mormon widows down this valley."

"Yes, I know about them." The corner of Grant's mouth threatened to curl in disgust.

"I want you to send your crews down there and fix their outer perimeter fences so your range cattle can't break in on their crops. Then I want you to pay them for whatever damage you've done to them, and last, I want you to pay them market price for their hay, grain, and produce that they want to sell for as long as you're in this valley."

"Then you will go look for my daughter?"

"I'm going to need some veteran Apache scouts." Slocum stood and rubbed his calloused hand over his mouth in deep consideration.

"They should arrive tonight. I sent word to the San Carlos agency yesterday I would need them."

"Need supplies, pack mules, two good skinners. Rifles, ammo. And we'll need extra."

"Extra? What does that mean?"

"You ain't getting any hostage back without ransom. If they shot Jericho and your foreman Manley with arrows they might consider arms in trade for your daughter."

Grant blinked in disbelief at him. "Can you get guns into Mexico?"

"You can get anything into Mexico if you have the money to bribe them or know where to slip across the border." Slocum rubbed his thumb and forefinger together. "That's no worry. But I'll be completely honest, Grant. The chances of finding your daughter alive down there are little to none."

"I will spare no expenses. Whatever you must do."

"Six scouts, you say, are coming." Slocum took a deep breath. No telling who they were. "Two mule skinners."

"I am certain I can find them around Bowie."

Slocum nodded. "We can leave in two days. When will you start your work on the widows' farms?"

"Tomorrow soon enough?"

"Fine, put Roy Gene here in charge."

The cowboy blinked at him and his boss.

"Fine with me," Grant said.

"You any kin to the ex-president?" Slocum asked.

"Distant, I think. Why?"

"There's enough resemblance."

"You knew President Grant?"

"No, but I saw him a few times."

"You an officer in the war?"

Slocum smiled. "I was on the other side."

Grant only nodded. "Roy can show you to your quarters. Supper is at seven."

"And I'd bet it will be grand, but I have other business to tend to."

"You will miss a brace of quail and a rib roast of corn-fed beef."

"Another time, perhaps. I'll be back here tomorrow night to decide who I take and don't take the next morning to Mexico out of those scouts you have coming."

"Slocum, find my daughter."

"I'll go look for her, Grant. It's a vast land that has many hiding places."

"Thank you," he said.

Hard thing for the pompous bastard to do was beg, Slocum decided and turned to leave.

"I'll get you a fresh horse," Roy Gene said, striding beside him for the front door.

"Fine idea, I may need Strawberry for the trip."

"Good day, Mr. Grant," the cowboy said at the door.

"Good day," the man said after them.

Slocum struck south on the fresh horse, a stout, long-legged bay. He loped him hard across the dusty flats of stirrup-high grass. His destination was Myra Downing's place. He carried good news for the widows of Sulfur Valley. They might not even believe him—it was that good. Their struggle against Grant would soon be over.

The bloody sun had dropped behind the Dragoons when he reined the lathered bay up at her front porch. He dropped heavily to the ground and his boot hung for an instant in the stirrup, then came free.

"That you, Slocum?" She stood in the lighted doorway, drying her hands on her apron.

"No, it's Brigham Young." He grinned at her in the twilight, undoing his latigoes.

"Ah, hell, it's you. Put that horse up and get in here."

"Yes, ma'am."

"I'll start you some supper, meanwhile."

Myra Downing stood under five foot tall. Amble hips and full breasts, she made what Slocum considered a bed full despite the shortness in height.

He tossed his saddle and pads on the corral, turned the bay in the lot where he could find water and feed after he rolled in the dust. Then Slocum struck out for the lighted house.

"What have you been up to?"

"Won a little at cards up at Freddie's. But I struck a deal for you and all your sisters."

"You did. With who?"

"Mr. Grant."

She turned and scowled at him. "What for?"

He began to tell her all the terms of his deal with Grant as he rested in a high-back wooden chair. Each time he told her another demand he had made, she looked up at the tin squares on the ceiling and said, "Amen, Lord."

Then after popping her pan of fresh-made biscuits into the range oven, she rushed over, clasped his face in both hands, and kissed him. In an instant, she climbed on his lap and their mouths were locked, her red-hot tongue seeking his like a thick snake. He molded her rock-hard breast with his right hand on top of the material.

Bleary eyed and out of breath, she tore her mouth away from his, sat up straight and undid the front buttons on her dress, then pushed his hand inside to touch her fiery flesh. Her nipple under his palm felt hard as a nail head as he skimmed over, fondling it. Kissing again, they went off into deep heady passion's throes.

"Oh, where have you been?" she moaned in his ear, catching her breath.

"Freddie's," he said, drunk with the rapture, and shoved the dress off her shoulders. He hoisted her up and began to suckle on the left nipple.

"Oh, dear God!" she screamed. "The bread!"

She jumped off his lap, grabbed some pot holders, and jerked the pan out of the oven. The pan of golden brown biscuits looked perfect to him as he stood behind her, reaching around to mold her breasts.

"They'll hold till later," she said and struggled out of the dress. Then, taking him by the hand, she led him to the bed in the corner of he room. Seated on the edge, she undid his belt and dropped his striped pants, then unbuttoned his underwear and freed his rock-hard shaft. Unable to wait a second longer she laid back on the edge of the bed, raised her legs in a V, and guided him in her wet gates.

Standing on the floor, he scooted closer, bent over and felt his throbbing dick go in past her ring. With her heels resting on his shoulders, he drove in his aching tool, and she cried out a loud, "Yes!"

Then her fingernails dug into his hatchet butt as she tried to pull him deeper and deeper inside the swollen, pulsating walls of her vagina. The bed's springs screamed in protest and she rocked on her back, using her toes to tease his ears. Her head was thrown back, her brown hair done up in a bun on the back of her head had came loose and spilled over the quilt as she cried for more.

He fought out of his vest and shirt and then stripped down the underwear, never missing a stroke. The cool night air ran over his bare skin as he fought to get into more of her with his legs bound in boots, pants, and underwear below his knees. Then a tingling feeling in the bottom of his balls began to gather. His efforts increased until the head of his dick felt ready to burst—then he gave a hard plunge so their pubic bones crashed together and he exploded inside her.

She screamed and clutched him.

To stand any longer required all of his effort. Dizzy headed, he pulled his sore dick out of her and swung around so he sat on the bed's edge, using his hands behind him to brace himself beside the collapsed Myra. At that point he realized that her legs were too short to even reach the floor. He noticed though they were hanging over the edge and she was still sprawled on her back.

"Hungry?" she asked in a dazed voice.

"Sure." He toed off his boots and then pulled off his pants and underwear.

"For what?"

"Get up on the bed and I'll show you."

"More?" she asked in a little voice.

Slocum grinned. "A lot more."

Soon she was on her knees and he came from behind her, reaching under to slide his member inside her. She gave a gasp, dropping down on her elbows as he began to pound her butt. Holding her pelvis bones in each hand, he was pouring his renewed erection into her. Then reaching underneath her, he began to mold her solid breasts and screw her faster.

From under a mantle of her freed hair, she shouted, "Don't ever stop!"

But he knew from the stirring in his sack it would only be a matter of seconds and he would come again. This time it felt like hot lava blowing out the head of his dick and she screamed—then fainted away under him.

He laid on his back and looked at the shadows from the flickering lamp dancing on the ceiling. "I have to go to Mexico and look for Grant's daughter or her remains."

"Is the whole U.S. Army going, too?" she asked, snuggled against him.

"No. Me and some Apache scouts Grant's hired and two mule skinners."

"You will need someone to cook." She used her thumb, pointing at her proud breasts.

"Too dangerous for you to go along." He shook his head.

She raised up on one elbow, traced her fingertip through the dark hair on his chest, and looked at him. "Not for me. Besides you will need someone to cook."

"I'll need lots of things—"

Her small fingers closed around his shaft and shut off his words. He felt the urge to lift his butt off the bed and meet her stroke. She began slow-like to jack him off. Then she rose on her knees, gave a toss of her long hair, and began kneading his scrotum with her other hand.

A grin on her full lips, she laughed out loud, then went back to her hand work. "You'd have made a great polygamist. You could have screwed them all once a night."

"Any word from your ex?"

She shook her head. "I think the church wants to send us down new husbands."

"Who are they?"

"Recruits they've gotten from England."

"When will they arrive?"

She tweaked his left nut, then grinned at him. "Why, are you worried?"

"Just asking." He closed his eyes to the intense pleasure of her caressing.

"I guess I could go get me a miner over at Tombstone. Or one of Ike Clanton's rustlers." Then she dropped her face down and her lips began to play on the rim of his dick's head. The sharp edges of her teeth grazed the tight skin and he knew he could not hold for long. Next her deep pulsating pull with her tongue on the underside and he came. Came hard.

She raised up, sweeping her long hair back. The white cream ran from the corner of her grinning mouth. "Jesus, that was neat."

He began to chuckle as she wiped the traces from her chin on her hand, looking frantic for something else to use.

"Man, why did Downing ever choose another woman over you?"

She wrinkled her nose and slipped off the bed. "He got in bed, crawled on, stuck it in me, two punches and then he grunted when he came. Sometime during the night he always woke up with a piss-filled one and wore me sore with it. It wasn't ever any fun."

"Business," Slocum said as he watched her firm breasts rise and fall as she scrubbed her face on a sack towel.

"It was all business to him. Keep his wives barefoot and pregnant."

"You never had any kids?"

"I couldn't carry them. He put me to bed on the last pregnancy. But it never made it."

"Sorry."

She shrugged, struggling to tie her hair back. "That's just the way it is. My gosh. I forgot all about your food."

Taking a robe down off a wall peg, she put it on and tied the belt around her waist. At the stove she tested the contents of a pot, then licked her finger. "The beans are still warm. Will that be enough with cold biscuits?"

"Sure," he said, pulling on his pants. Seated on the edge of the bed, he rubbed an itch on his upper lip and his actions released her strong musk residues up his nostrils.

"I can't wait to tell the others about your deal. You think he'll really do it?"

"Yeah, he'll have to or lose face. He'll send this bashful cowboy around whose name's Roy Gene. I think he's a virgin."

"How old is he?"

"Midtwenties."

"Oh, will they have fun with him."

"I figured that."

She brought him a tin plate heaped with beans and biscuits as well as a spoon.

While he ate, she told him about the other gossip in the valley. What she knew about Clanton's and Laughery's rustling business, the Earp's order of law over in Tombstone, and how one of the widows, Freda Cross, had a long dong rustler named Robbie Ebons frequenting her bed.

"She swears he's got sixteen inches of dick."

Slocum laughed. "That would be enough."

"Lordy, you could do it from across the room with one that long." They both laughed. Then she fretted over her small hands in her lap, not looking up when she spoke. "I want to go along and see that country down there."

"It'll be dangerous as hell. There's some of Ho's old band left down there. It wouldn't be pretty you being a squaw or gang-banged by a whole mob of them steel-dicked bucks."

"I still want to go."

"All right, you can go along. Who'll watch your place?"

"Margie Langdon's boy Mark. He's fifteen and dependable. When do you leave?"

"Wednesday morning."

She nodded. "I'll be ready. Want more food?"

"No," he said, rubbing his belly. "I just want to lay here on the bed and fart."

"Just like a man," she said, taking his dishes and shaking her head.

Slocum sprawled back on the bed, finding a pillow and looking at the ceiling's tin tiles. No talking her out of going—she was dead set. He hoped he could protect her from harm up there, but he wasn't certain he could take care of himself let alone her.

In a minute, she was back scrambling around on the bed top, undoing his pants, pulling them off, and then fighting off the robe as she knelt on all fours beside him.

"Your friend got another in him?"

"Maybe." Then they both laughed.

3

Slocum looked over the six Apaches squatted in the shade of the shed. Three wore Mexican straw sombreros to shade their dark faces; the other half had only headbands. They acknowledged him with a nod when he spoke to them in Spanish. All were Apaches. That part of Grant's actions, he approved of—the other tribes couldn't light a candle to the scouting an Apache could do, especially tracking their own kind.

He dropped to his boot heels to squat in front of them, used a stick to mark in the dust. "A half dozen bucks run off from San Carlos, robbed a stage, killed the driver, guard, and kidnapped a girl." He tossed his head toward the big house. "His daughter. He wants her back."

The somber head nods around the half circle told him they already knew the details.

"She still alive, Silver Bar?" he asked the scout he knew best in the group.

"Long ways to Mother mountains."

"Caychem?" he asked the younger one.

Thinner-faced, handsome-looking, he shook his head. "Don't know."

"Maybe Chee killed her."

Slocum shook his head. "Who is he?"

"She. Jericho's woman at the stage station. She went with them."

"Why?" Slocum asked.

"She was One Deer's woman."

"How come was she with Jericho?"

The scout talking laughed and showed his white, even teeth. "So she could steal all old man's money."

19

"Who are you?"

"Call me Tom."

"Okay, Tom. So this woman Chee stole all his money. Why?"

"Money talks big in Mexico. Even Apaches know about money now. They use to pour it out. Hope the gold it came from would go back the ground. Not now. Money will buy them even protection down there."

"Good," Slocum said. "We leave at daybreak and ride to the border. We will cross into Mexico and not be seen."

The scouts acknowledged his plan.

"The one who really leads them is Wolf," the talkative scout Tom said.

"Who's he?"

"They say he is a son of Victorio."

"Warm Springs?" Slocum asked. He knew that the Warm Springs and Chiricuhuas were closely related through marriages over the years. The old chief Cochise had been married to Victorio's sister before his death.

Tom nodded and the others spoke in their own guttural language.

"What we don't find her?" Caychem asked, in his broken English.

"We come home and throw a big drunk."

The dark face broke into a grin. "We find her, we have a bigger one."

"Right." They all laughed.

Slocum heard the mules before he even rounded the corner of the pens. He blinked his eyes. Seated on his ass in the dirt, swigging whiskey out of a quart that the sun glinted off was Posey Conrad. Had he been downwind, Slocum would have smelled the bath-less old goat in his grimy, once-tan clothing and floppy brimmed straw hat.

"Son of a bitch, if it ain't you after all." Conrad made an effort to get up, using his hand behind his back on the corral rails, and at the same time tried to drink from the neck.

"I said, 'Why you're lying to me boy,' when that scalawag that you sent over to Bowie came to tell me that Slocum was leading this fucking outfit. 'Hell'—he teetered on his flat boot heels and blinked his rheumy looking eyes at Slocum—"that sum bitch Slocum is dead by now.'"

"You had a bath lately, Conrad?"

"Hell, no, and precious as water as in this hellhole I ain't taking one either."

"You're either going to go take a bath or you ain't going with us."

"You gawdamn sure ain't big enough to make me take one." He put down his whiskey and began to put up his fists.

Slocum stepped in, blocked his first punch, and drove a haymaker to his gut that sent all the wind out of Conrad in one long outward rush. He keeled over face-first. Slocum turned to the three Indians standing behind him.

"Put him in that irrigation ditch around there for starters."

They nodded. One on each arm, the other buck on his kicking feet, they carted him around the pen, and soon Slocum heard a splash followed by a scream like someone was dying. The mules in the pen all looked sound and good size to Slocum. There was another shout—his scouts must have reinserted Conrad in the water from the sounds.

"Damn, I'm glad I ain't on your list."

"Roman Jones," Slocum said recognizing the coarse drawl.

"This pretty much a wild goose chase?" Jones asked.

Slocum looked over the short, broad-built skinner. He looked stout as ever. "The man has the money. He wants his daughter back. Word is these bucks understand money and what it will buy them."

"What have you got figured?"

"I'm taking some extra repeating rifles with us, in case they'll trade her for them. That's why we're having to slip into Mexico."

"Heading for the Sierra Madres, right?"

"Right."

"What if they want ten thousand dollars?"

"Reckon a damn Apache can count that high?" He smiled at the mule man.

Jones shook his head. "Who knows?"

"I say we can go look. I never promised him a thing, but that. Personally I think she's liable to be already dead by this time."

"Them bucks over there may drown old Conrad. They threw him in again." Jones climbed on the corral so he could see the fracas.

"This ain't funny, you gawdamn red niggers!" Conrad screamed.

The three scouts looked across the corral to Slocum when he stood halfway up on the fencing. With a nod, he gave them a shooing wave and they grinned—turning back to their work.

"Oh, no!" Conrad wailed. "Slocum, you bastard, I'll get you too."

Slocum went past the jacal assigned to him by a matronly white woman, Mrs. Daggett, who acted in charge. He stopped in the commissary doorway and removed his hat to wipe the perspiration off his face on his sleeve. Inside, Myra was busy working on the panniers stored in the room.

"What's happening?" Slocum asked.

"The scouts and skinners are eating at the ranch table tonight and again in the morning to give us an earlier start," Myra said.

"How did the supplies check out?"

"Good enough. I had them put on some more airtight cans of peaches and tomatoes. Boys love them. Some of that water between here and there ain't fit to drink."

"You've been down there?"

"Yeah, I lived for three years at Colonias, the Mormon settlement where all the polygamous went."

"That's in the foothills, right?"

"Yeah."

"Why did you leave?"

"Downing couldn't make enough money down there. All he ever thought about was making money and babies."

"He make money?"

"Yeah, because he had all his wives and kids farming like slaves."

"So much for the good life."

She nodded. "What was the damn screaming about?"

"My scouts gave Posey Conrad a couple of baths."

"Who's he?" A frown knitted her thin brows together.

"Some old bath-less mule skinner."

"He ain't eating my food smelling like some old goat, nor is he getting around me."

"I'll tell him."

"Sooner he knows the better. I was fixing to take a siesta. What're you doing next?" She gave him a seductive smile.

He swatted her playfully on the butt. "Telling Conard how the deal works."

"What'll he say?"

"Oh, he'll want to have another fistfight."

"Better you fight him than me."

"He ain't hard to whip, you just have to do it so often that it gets tiring."

"After that if you get horny come by my swing." She held her hand out to the hammock.

"I may do that—I just may." He kissed her on the lips and headed out past the blanket hanging over her door.

Conrad could either go to town and get cleaned up or not go.

In the midday heat, Slocum started for the main house. If Albert Grant wasn't napping, he wanted some last-minute words with the man.

The Mexican houseboy showed him inside and took him to the rear of the large room. A smell of new plaster filled the air, and some workers were standing on scaffolds working on the high ceiling.

"Well, how does it go?" Grant asked.

"Fine. Well arranged."

"They tell me one of the Mormon widows is going along to cook for them."

"Myra Downing. I'll pay her."

"No." Grant looked up at the work going on above them. "I'll pay her like the rest. You plan to leave early?"

"We'll eat breakfast at four and pull out. I want to rest until dark up in the Mule Shoes where it's cool for few hours, then hit the desert and cross into Sonora in the night."

"Good plan. I like to research most of the men I hire above common laborers." Grant crossed his arms. "You have any inky past, Slocum?"

"You didn't hire me because I was some Indian War hero."

"No, I wanted someone who stood a chance to get my daughter back."

"What did you need to know?"

"I think Texas John Slaughter told me all I needed to know. Down at the San Bernadino Ranch, you know him?"

Slocum nodded.

"He said it's a toss-up—who you get makes no difference. Al Sieber, Tom Horn, or you."

"John flattered me. That's tough company."

"Delightful man."

Slocum agreed about Slaughter. "I came one more time to tell you, it could save you some money if we didn't go down there."

Grant narrowed his eyes. "If I thought I had not done everything possible to get my daughter back, I'd probably never sleep again."

"Fine, but this one is a long shot."

"I appreciate your concern and I respect your experience and knowledge of these people, but go and do what you can—Slocum, if they have murdered my girl, I will pay five thousand dollars for her killer's head."

Slocum could read the torment in the man's look as he tried to act interested in the plastering going on high overhead. He'd sent his best man to retrieve his daughter from a stage—simple enough—instead the man was dead and his daughter kidnapped by angry Apaches. With all of his wealth, he'd never have let it happen if he could have prevented it.

Slocum thought about the hammock. "I'm going to take a siesta."

"Good idea—" Grant's eyes narrowed. "If you can sleep."

4

The eastern star shown bright off toward Lordsburg, New Mexico Territory. In the cool hours before the sun rose and blasted the land, men, and their braying mules, they struggled to get loaded.

"Meet us at the summit of the pass," Slocum said to his skinners. "We'll water them at Sutter's place up there. Rest till late in the night then head south."

"See you there," Jones said.

Slocum nodded to them and led the way out the gate. Caychem was leading the way. He'd already rode ahead to find the best way to trail along the bottom of the Chiricuhuas and then up on Mule Pass. When they got in Mexico, Slocum would use the scouts as flankers on both sides to keep the main party out of harm's way. For now he was only testing his main man's skills to lead them.

Superstitious as Apaches were about night he knew they always were edgy until the sun came up. They believed anyone killed at night was denied an afterlife. Caychem kept them to the flat country. Slocum noticed the horses made little dust even when the sun finally climbed over the backbone of the Chiricuhuas. Myra rode a short mountain-bred horse—the kind of one appreciated in the stiff uphill rides they'd make in the Madres. Good dispositioned and powerful, his kind skimmed those narrow trails sure-footed as a goat.

"Will we get into Mexico all right?" she asked.

"Yes, there shouldn't be much word about us until we are across the border going like we are. If we'd hung around either at Grant's or down there for very long the border cantina talk would have made it common knowledge."

"Almost like a telegraph?"

"Yes and they may know we're coming anyway. Not much is a secret in Mexico."

Midday, they reached Paul Sutter's place. His wooden-framed windmill's flashing blades creaked in the wind, pumping cool water into the huge rock-mortar tank.

"Hello hombre," the big tall Texan said, striding down from his snug house to meet them. "Long time no see. What have you here?" He squinted against the sun's glare and noted the half dozen mounted Apaches.

"Need a little water," Slocum said. "Good to see you. This is Myra."

The Texan swept off his hat and bowed. "My pleasure, ma'am. I seldom receive such beauty and grace at my place. May I offer you the uncomforts of my abode?"

She looked at Slocum and he nodded, then removed his own hat and wiped the sweat off his forehead. The cooler wind swept his face. This was a good choice and obviously the tall man in his lace-up boots was fascinated by her. *Not hard to be*, he decided, dropping heavily from the saddle.

"Go with him," Slocum said. "I'll water your horse."

Sutter showed her the crook of his arm and led her off after Slocum gave her a reassuring nod and caught the reins. Might be the last time for weeks she could enjoy some comforts. He looked off to the south and wondered what he'd find in Mexico. Always an adventure down there, sometimes disastrous, but an adventure. The only problem was he led a small army on a fool's mission. Amantha Grant probably lay dead somewhere between Jehrico's stage stop and the border by his calculation.

He jerked the latigoes loose on both saddles and Caychem took the reins.

"We rest here amigo until late tonight," he said to the Apache in the red headband.

"Apaches know how to rest. I am going to scout the way. There is an Apache woman lives in the country south of here, who may know something about the girl. I want to speak to her."

"Going to take anyone?"

"The boy Cooty. She is his sister and married a Mexican."

Slocum agreed. "Be careful."

The scout agreed and went with the two horses to join the rest of his scouts around the tank.

At the house, Slocum stopped in the doorway.

"Come in," Sutter said. "Myra and I were just talking. This man Grant has offered ten thousand dollars for the return of his daughter alive."

Slocum closed his eyes to cringe. Grant had never mentioned offering any reward. This would sure blotch up his own plans. Ten thousand American was a fortune in Mexico, not to mention the U.S.

"That's lots of money. You could hold up half the banks in Sonora and not get that much," Sutter said.

"You're right. That means every two-bit bandit in Mexico is on the lookout for her, plus who knows who else."

Sutter brought him a glass of whiskey. "I figured you'd need this."

"That and some more." He raised his glass to him and Myra seated on the couch.

"People may be falling all over each other down there looking for her."

"You could be right. What worries me more than that is some outlaw finds her alive and then he asks for even more."

Sutter turned from the table with a glass of liquor for himself and nodded with a serious look on his face. "You may have a rough time."

"Nothing ever came easy. We get paid, win, lose, or draw."

"Don't forget," she said, with smug look, holding her right knee in the divided riding skirt and rocking on her butt. "You did make a deal for the widows of Sulfur Valley."

Sutter searched the two of them. "What's that?"

"The seven widows—you know about the polygamy thing. Well, seven of the wives that are running places of their own down there are now under his protection."

"Let's drink to that," Sutter said and he raised his glass. "I had no idea there were seven eligible women down there."

"Don't let it keep you away," Myra said.

"It won't." He turned to Slocum. "That reward business change your plans?"

"No, I figured I'd have surprises."

"You think she's still alive?"

Slocum looked out the open front door toward the distant purple Huchuchas. "Be a miracle."

"My thoughts exactly. Now Myra, tell me about your place?" Sutter moved in and sat beside her on the cowhide couch.

From the elk and deer antlers on the wall to the Navajo rugs on the tile floor, Sutter's place showed some sign of his prosperity. Some he made in the cattle drives out of Texas, others in his mining ventures; some said he had a gold vein on his place, which he kept secret. Slocum knew the small herd of cattle he ran in the Mule Shoes were not the source of his wealth. Their friendship went back a decade when living up there was a real threat to survival in the path of Geronimo and others' retreats into Mexico.

Sutter never denied the Apaches access to his water. When General Miles demanded he allow some of the black troopers from Fort Huchuchas to guard the tank from the Apaches' use of it, he'd told Miles's lieutenant no. He'd survived the traipsing of the renegades and had no wish to upset them. So instead, the buffalo soldiers were stationed on both sides of his ranch to cover the route.

Despite the military's show of force, there still were at times the small imprints of their pointed-toe knee-high boots in the soft dirt around the tank. Individuals moving like the wind back and forth between the hostiles' camp in Mexico and the reservation.

"You have mules and all?" Sutter asked.

Slocum nodded. "We came equipped. They'll be here before dark."

"Is it good to be back in the saddle?" Sutter asked, obviously more interested in talking to Myra than him.

Slocum nodded. The man didn't realize how much time he'd spent on the move the past few years after Geronimo's surrender, looking over his shoulder for a bounty hunter or the two Abbott Brothers from Fort Scott, Kansas. With or without Grant's project, it had been time for him to leave this country anyway and move on.

He agreed to another refill of his glass. *Quite a place Sutter owned on top of this mountain. How big was his vein of gold?*

5

Two days later, Slocum'd watched the bank of clouds build all morning in the southwest. They were pushing the mules hard to reach Rio Maria, a small village in the foothills, where he felt they could stay safe enough overnight.

"Be lots of dust in that storm?" Myra asked, riding beside him as the wind picked up.

Caychem came riding in, taking ominous looks over his shoulder. "There is an abandoned place ahead. We can wait out the storm there."

Slocum agreed and rode back to tell the skinners and the scouts busy helping drive the mules faster. By this time he had to shout over the wind and the stinging sand blasted his face. The solemn Apaches nodded in agreement and the two skinners made grim faces that they'd heard him as they jerked along their resistant string. The mules had no desire to go into the strong wind and only by stout lead horses and the scouts with their quirts beating on them did they even move at all.

Visibility soon dissolved into a brown world of swirling dirt, and seeing beyond a few yards became impossible. Slocum shouted for her to stay close to the train and used his lariat to punish the mules close by into hurrying. His bandana over his mouth, his eyes were bombarded by diamond-like particles that caused him to ride with his head down and hope they were going the right way.

They dropped into a wash and crossed it. The dim outline of buildings loomed before them and he shouted for her to get inside the first one.

"Take your horse in too!"

She nodded, and holding down her wide-brimmed straw hat, she leaned into the force. Soon she and her mount disappeared inside the first jacal. They fought with the mules, but the double doors of the former cantina were wide and tall enough to allow the braying jackasses access without unloading them. The task was whip and drag to get them indoors. In all the effort, one reared and broke loose from one of the scouts leading him. Wheeling around, Slocum worried for a moment it might run off, but it quit short of flight, not wanting to leave its mates. Caught again, then with shouting, cussing, and whipping, he soon joined the others inside.

"Unload?" someone asked him over the howling wind outside.

Slocum nodded. Myra had joined them and she headed the unpacking operation, so she could find her food and utensils. His arms full with a pannier, Slocum heard the first drops of mud on the roof, grateful to be inside. It would rain bloody mud for thirty minutes and then maybe quit. He could recall once being out in it when the flushing rain never did come after the initial mud bath and he dried out like an adobe brick.

The mules were finally unloaded. The men sprawled out on the floor, listening to the thunder roll over the desert and the flushing rain outside filling the depressions with water. It looked like they had found a place to stay for the night.

Myra sent them after some firewood between streaks of rain for her cooking and soon she had coffee for all of them. *Not bad tasting either*, Slocum decided, *for someone who never drank it*. He blew the steam off his first cup and squatted on his boot heels.

She diced up bacon for her beans and turned her head to listen for the next approaching storm. "More's coming."

"In waves," he agreed.

"In the desert it's always good to have rain."

"Always, cause the next one may be two years away."

She laughed. "Or longer than that. Will we camp in one place in the mountains?"

"Yes, I hope to make a base camp. We should be there in two more days."

As if she had no worries about it, she shrugged and busied herself chopping the bacon. "Then what?"

"Be up to these Apaches to find her—"

A shrill whistle sent everyone in the cantina going for their guns. Slocum rushed for the front door. He could hear horses and riders coming. His scouts went every direction out the doors.

Conrad and Jones, armed with Winchesters, were there with him.

"Can you see them?" Jones asked.

"Ain't the gawdamn federales," Conrad swore. "They don't talk all the time like these are doing."

Slocum agreed with the man's observation; by then he could see the first riders. They were either bandits or fortune hunters. The lead rider wore a black beard and halted his crew of perhaps a dozen riders.

"Wait here," he said in Spanish and rode his wet gray horse forward. He wore bandoleers, half full of ammo, crisscross over his chest and held a rifle balanced on his leg as he approached Slocum, who was standing in the doorway.

"It looks like more rain is coming."

Slocum nodded. "My name is Slocum."

"And mine is Phillipe."

"Good to meet you."

The man wiped his mustache, then his beard down with the web of his hand. "We will use the old store if that suits you?"

"Fine," Slocum said, glancing up to see the armed Apaches begin to appear on the rooftops. "It's all right," he said to settle the aroused-looking Phillipe. "They work for me."

"Good. That was hard on my heart." He waved the other riders in with his arm.

Like they had appeared, the scouts disappeared from the roofs nearby when the half dozen riders rode by him. Slocum saw Phillipe's men were mostly young ranch hands, and only one looked like a tough one. He gave Slocum a hard look and a sharp nod as he rode by the cantina.

One of the young ones asked Slocum if he had anything to drink inside.

Slocum shook his head and smiled. The others laughed as they dismounted and then hurried inside before the next band of rain swept in. When Slocum returned to Myra, she had the bacon browned and added it to the pot of beans.

Caychem joined him—squatted down and looked hard eyed at the small fire under her pots.

"Coffee?" Slocum asked, reaching for a cup for him.

The scout nodded.

"You know them?"

The Apache shook his head. "There are two men trailing them."

"Who are they?" Slocum shifted on his toes as he squatted on the ground to look at his man.

"Bad hombres."

Slocum listened to the hard rain on the roof. The various leaks began to drip. They could not expect much better for free.

"Why do you think they follow them?"

Caychem shrugged. "They don't look rich enough to rob."

Slocum agreed and listened to the thunder roll. "Can we take these *malo* hombres prisoners?"

The fast smile on the Apache's face almost made Slocum laugh out loud. Caychem held his cup out for Myra to spoon in sugar. They liked it thick with sweetness. "We'll catch them."

"Take your time," Slocum said and went back for his own. She'd poured him a fresh cup too.

"This may be interesting," she said and gave him an elbow.

Slocum agreed. He'd learned that Cooty's sister knew nothing about the girl's welfare. The story they brought back from her was the last thing she knew: Amantha Grant was still alive and with the renegades headed for the Mother mountains. All second and thirdhand rumors—part of what Slocum considered the desert wireless telegram that usually bore some assemblance of the true thing. In fact, the notion that she still might be alive had shattered his belief about her real fate. If she lived any time at all amongst them, then she could well survive. Those first days were crucial. Though sometimes the harshness of their ways caused their captives to lose their sanity under the duress and they became the walking dead.

He recalled Sonja Guetenberg, taken by the Comanches on the Brazos River. A sixteen-year-old washing clothes on the bank when they captured her. Her younger sister of twelve was raped by several bucks in her sight, then they savagely killed the sister when she wouldn't quit screaming. Three days later after repeated gang rapes, a young warrior took Sonja as his wife. She no longer talked, simply rode her horse that he led and she hung on. A week later, naked, she wandered away from them and was found by two rangers. The two young men cut a hole in one of their blankets to make a dress for her and carried her back to Buena Grande. A relative took her in, and she sat on the porch every day rocking in a chair and humming a Comanche song. She never spoke to any of them. Never did any housework or offered to help do a thing. She sat and hummed out of her nose. Then one day, an Indian wearing only a loincloth and a greasy eagle feather in his hair rode up to the yard picket fence. As if on signal, she rushed off the porch, took his arm, swung up behind him, and they left in a dead run. Family members spent months looking for her, but not a trace was ever found.

Ten years later, near Fort Sill, Oklahoma, where the Comanches finally went to be on a reservation, someone recognized a squaw among them as her. Sonja had several small half-breed children of her own at the time and no desire to leave her Comanche husband. Fluent in his language, she spoke some English to them. However, they said most of the time she still hummed a song that they didn't know, but suspected it as the same one she'd hummed on the porch of her relatives in north Texas.

Slocum wondered about Amantha Grant. *Was she still sane?* He noticed in the dark room the mules shifting around nervous-like all in a line over there—four scouts were also gone.

Myra made sourdough biscuits in a Dutch oven and when they came out she tossed him one. "They're hot."

She smiled at him, and the others gathered around her as she opened the lid on a jar, filled with dark desert honey.

"You're going to spoil us," Slocum said around the first bite of his biscuit—delicious.

He looked up and saw two hatless Mexican males in their late twenties or so were being shoved through the backdoor of the building under heavy guard of his scouts. Hands bound behind their back, from the looks of their clothing they had been in a fight that they'd lost.

"These are the ones I spoke about," Caychem said, indicating them with the muzzle of his Winchester.

"What's your business here?" Slocum asked the shorter one with the mustache.

He shrugged and looked around like he wasn't telling nothing.

"They tell me Apaches like to eat roasted nuts. 'Cept they don't take them off you before the roast them."

"Apaches?" Wide eyed, he glanced around at the scouts.

"They're Apaches," Slocum assured the two.

"We don't know you," the prisoner said quickly. His partner, with his shoulder almost touching him by this time to be further away from the scouts, shook his head too.

"Why're you following them then?"

"My boss he tell me to."

"Who's your boss?"

"Victor Hernandez."

"You know why he sent you to follow them."

"No, I swear on the Virgin Mary, I know nothing." He ducked his head as if in fear of being struck.

"What did he tell you to look for?"

"The girl."

"What girl?"

"The one with the yellow hair."

"Where is she?"

The prisoner shook his head and indicated the others in the village. "They don't have her yet."

"They going to have her?"

"I think so."

"What're you going to do with these two?" Myra asked him privately.

"I'm not sure. Maybe go talk to Phillipe."

"Be careful."

"I will. Put them in the corner for now," he said to the scouts. "We can roast their balls later." He exchanged a private smile with Caychem.

The rain had stopped and Slocum walked over to the store. Phillipe met him on the front porch.

"You know a Victor Hernandez?" Slocum asked, looking across the puddles in the depressions that dotted the street.

"He's a bad hombre. Why?"

"He thinks you know where the yellow-haired girl is at."

The man frowned at Slocum. "Who?"

"He said the yellow-haired girl. His men said you knew where she was at." Slocum folded his arms over his chest.

"I wish I did. I would love to collect the ten thousand dollars reward."

Slocum nodded. "Any idea?"

"I wanted to go look for her in the mountains."

"You headed there?" Slocum asked.

"Yes, but I have to get some supplies first. But you have plenty of supplies, no?"

"Barely enough for my crew to last a few weeks on it." Grant's reward business worried him more than his own supplies at the moment. The bounty would get the girl killed if nothing else had happened to her—all these treasure hunters looking for her. All they'd do was make her renegade captors more careful and more treacherous.

"When did you talk to his men?" Phillipe asked.

"A few minutes ago. They've been tracking you. My scouts caught them."

Phillipe shook his head in disgust at the knowledge. "Hernandez is a very bad hombre. But I am grateful you caught his men."

"I intend to let them go—barefoot—when we leave here."

"Probably better than cutting their throats."

"We may wish I'd done that too."

"I will try to stay out of your way, senor. I do not wish to arouse your ire or the Apache scouts'."

"Free country."

"I am grateful for you telling me about the spies."

"No problem."

Slocum was not satisfied that when push came to shove Phillipe wouldn't try to take the girl away from them if they did manage to find her alive. Walking back to the cantina he wondered how many more in Mexico wouldn't do the same. Grant's damn reward would be the death of him yet. He looked at the fiery sundown. Maybe he'd feel better up in the Madres—for the moment, he felt nauseated about the entire deal.

Even Myra noticed his concern when he returned and she brought him a plate of food. "Did the meeting not go good over there?"

"Not that, but all of Mexico is getting the damn reward fever for that girl. It isn't good and we're right in the damn middle."

"Eat your supper. You and these Apaches will figure it out."

"I sure in the hell hope so."

6

Mules brayed and the entire crew drove them hard. The day before's rain had already evaporated. Bitter acrid dust boiled up, but there was nothing he could do about that. He knew anyone who wanted to watch his movements could simply do so with a telescope or field glasses, but shortly he aimed to be more concealed in the foothills. His advance scouts had found nothing when they reported in at midday.

"Where will this Wolf take them?"

"Rio Blanca," Caychem said.

"I thought so too. Can we be close to there in another day?"

The Apache nodded. "You want a couple of us to head up there and see if they are there?"

"Yes, but be careful. You could get caught in a cross-fire."

"Cross-fire?"

"I mean you get between the renegades and someone like Hernandez, you might be in a tight place."

"We will watch our backs. How many should I take with me?"

"How many do you need?"

"Three."

"Pick them and the other three can get out front and be certain we don't ride into an ambush."

"Tom is a good one to scout ahead."

"Fair enough. You tell him where you have been this morning and get some food from her to take along with the ones you choose."

"There is good place to camp in the mountains."

"That's where we will be in a day and a half?"

The scout agreed.

36

Myra, overhearing his words, rushed off to get from the panniers some jerky and dried fruit for the scouts to carry with them. Slocum looked at the towering purple mass of the mountains rising in the east like castles. To escape the desert's stifling heat and feel a cool breeze on his face would be a welcome relief.

After the noon break they pressed on, reaching a spring and some grass for the stock in the foothills. Slocum was pleased with their day's progress. His mule skinners even acted human-like when they finished unpacking.

"Ma'am," Posey said with his hat wadded in his hand. "I never had much faith in bringing along a woman to cook, but I reckon that was the smartest thing ole Slocum ever done."

"Why thank you, Posey, I take that as a compliment."

"Yeah, do that. 'Cause I mean it."

Slocum walked over where she was working over the fire and smiled when she filled his coffee cup. "Even winning over that old coot."

She looked off down the camp where the skinner had gone. "Hell, that ain't hard, he never had any good food on the trail and when he was in town he was drunk and couldn't taste a thing."

They both laughed.

"We'll be at that camp tomorrow?" she asked.

"Hope to be. We'll throw up a fly tent. Got enough canvas for that when we get there."

"Been lucky we haven't got more afternoon rains."

"It's that season. We'll get more afternoon showers in the mountains." He looked off toward the high county that towered above them and knew that thunderstorms were wetting them down.

Tom returned before dark. He'd left his two scouts on the trail above them, and rode in alone. His return alone bothered Slocum, so he went to meet his man.

"What's wrong?"

"I think someone is ahead of us. Maybe three horses. Two are shod. I think the other is a packhorse. He is barefoot."

"Not Cayhem's tracks?" Slocum asked as they squatted in the gathering darkness near the campfire.

"No, I saw them—they are further from the trail than these were."

"No law against going into the Madres. What has you so upset?"

"Sometimes an owl will hoot in the daytime and tell you something. When I looked at those tracks an owl hooted twice."

"So you think we've been warned?"

Tom nodded.

"Better get some food for yourself and then take some to the boys on the trail. I'll keep my eyes open."

"Trouble?" Myra asked, returning to her dishes after she fed Tom and made some food up for him to take to the others.

"Superstitious Injuns. I hope he's wrong, but he thinks someone ahead of us is out to hurt us."

Up to her elbows in soapsuds, she nodded. "I hope he's wrong too. But I knew that this wasn't going to be a Sunday school picnic."

"Not hardly," Slocum agreed. "And Grant didn't make it any easier either."

"I sure hope he's fixing my fences. That boy'll have his hands full enough irrigating the hay while I'm gone."

"Grant ain't, I'll kick his ass."

She laughed. "I believe you'd do that."

Slocum carried his .44/40 Winchester in the crook of his arm. The mule skinners and Myra were in their bedding in the shadows of some cottonwoods. Stars and the quarter moon kept the rest of the surrounding valley in a pearly light, so he could see anyone coming long before they got to them or the mules. Squatted down with his back to a rough-barked cottonwood he surveyed the land around them.

A red wolf howled and a mate answered along the ridge above him. Looking for mule deer, they soon were gone over the hill. That also meant there was no one on that side or the carnivores would not have shown themselves. The mules and horses went back to grazing. They would see or hear someone before he did, raise their heads, and watch the intruder. He relied a lot on animals to telegraph the approach of strangers. Many times the sight of a horse peering off into the night saved his neck. His horse once saw a bounty man creeping up a long time before he ever got to Slocum.

He slept some, seated on the ground, then he awoke and checked all signs, horses, and the area. Not anything out of place. He shut his eyes and dozed again. It proved harder to wake up the next time. Like a man drowning in a deeper whirlpool, out of breath and struggling for the surface, he at last opened his eyelids and saw three figures afoot, running low, headed for the mules and horses. No time to try to take aim in the dim light, he fired the rifle in the air to wake the rest of the camp.

The three sneaks stopped and began running back for the dark security of the trees. With them at least away from the horses, he opened fire. Of course, his shots were taken without much sighting due to the lack of sufficient light. But the night soon was filled with rifle shots as the Apaches joined him. One of the escaping raiders screamed; he was hit.

Good! Maybe they could learn something from him. They weren't Apache renegades—their words had been in Spanish. Probably some more fortune seekers out to collect Grant's reward. But why try to steal his stock? Maybe so him and his bunch couldn't continue. Slocum hurried to find Myra. She no doubt would be shaken by all the shooting. He could see the Apache scouts were in hot pursuit of the would-be rustlers.

"What's happening?" Roman Jones asked, with his rifle ready.

"Think we about had some attempted horse and mule stealing," Slocum said, looking off toward the brush and scrub junipers where the scouts had disappeared.

"Sonsabitches!" Conrad swore, shaking his head. "Wake a man up having the dream about the best piece of ass in his life."

"Might have been his last, too," Slocum said and headed for where Myra slept among the panniers.

"Myra?" he called out when he drew close to them.

"All clear?" she asked in a sleep-husky voice and appeared with a pistol in her hand.

"I think so. Three guys were sneaking up on the horses when I woke up awhile ago. I shot at them, to scare them off, and the Apaches have gone after them."

She yawned big and then shook her head. "Damn I was sleeping good. I better get a fire going—this bunch will be hungry in a little while."

He gave her shoulder a hug and kissed her on the mouth. "Sorry."

"Hey, I asked to come along."

"Good, it sure won't be peaches and cream."

She put her arm around his waist and squeezed him. "Up until now it has been fun. Beats sitting at home or cutting hay."

Tom brought back the wounded outlaw. Him and Trigger set the man on the ground.

"What's your name?' Slocum asked, squatting down to talk to him.

"Sorento—Manuel Sorento."

"Manuel, who do you work for?"

"No one—"

"Manuel, I don't want to ask questions twice. I'll let the Apaches have you. You'll answer their questions. You savvy, hombre?"

"*Si*, Hernandez sent me."

"To do what?"

"Cripple some of your horses and mules."

"To slow us down?"

"*Si.*"

"Where is Hernandez?"

"Fronteras, I guess."

"When were you to meet him?"

"He never said."

"Let me have that pip-squeak. He'll be talking like a hen that just laid an egg in couple of minutes," Conrad put in. "I'll put his nuts in a vise and smash them one at a time."

"I don't know—" Manuel screamed, obviously pained by the wound in his shoulder.

Slocum ignored the mule skinner's suggestion and looked at Tom. "Did Silver Bar go after the others?"

"Yes. He took one of their horses to follow them."

"You two better go help him. It may be a trap."

"But what about you and the others?"

"We won't start out until we hear from you."

Tom gave a head toss to Trigger and they left on the run for their horses.

Slocum wheeled around on his haunches and looked at Sorento. "Why did Hernandez need more time?"

"He never said."

"Oh, you must know something."

"His main man Don Corallis was to meet us in two days."

"Where?"

"A place called Calienta Pass." Manuel hugged his arm to his wounded side and winced.

Slocum nodded, then glanced up at the two mule skinners.

They shook their heads—neither of them knew of a place so named. Was he lying? No, Slocum doubted it. Maybe one of the Apaches knew where he meant. Maybe the ones ahead that Cay-chem looked for was this Corallis and his men. No telling. Then Manuel fainted.

Standing at last, Slocum told Jones to tie the outlaw's feet so when he awoke he couldn't run off. The mule skinner nodded he would and went for some rope.

Myra had coffee ready when he walked over to the fire, busy going through his mind about what to do next.

"Coals were still hot," she said, pouring him some in a tin cup. "What do you know now?"

"Not much. More troublemakers hired by Hernandez."

"He's getting to be a real pain in the"—she looked around to be certain no one heard her—"a real pain in the ass." Then she slapped her own rump and laughed.

"I agree. I can't seem to find a way to nip him off at the bud."

"You'll figure one out."

"I hope so." He looked off at the towering range of the Madres above them. In another hour it would be daylight. They'd need to have the mules packed and be ready to move by then. When Tom and his two scouts got back, they'd start up the mountain. Up there they'd have cooler weather, monsoonal showers in the afternoon, and maybe even find Amantha Grant. If she was still alive.

7

Thunder rolled across the mountainside. Slocum and Myra were helping drive the mules faster by riding in and beating on them. They could all rest when they made camp. Still another mile or so according to the Apache scout. Tom said the valley they wanted to make camp in was only a short ways ahead. The ominous dark cloud over Slocum's shoulder bearing down on them looked like an icy bath for his crew.

They finally reached the open valley, and Slocum could see it was grass-covered and the stock would be fine there. Icy drops of rain began to pepper his back. It would be cold as the Arctic in minutes. Myra shook out a canvas coat and fought to put it on. The three scouts huddled under some pines. Slocum wished for a slicker, but more than that wondered where his other three scouts were at. Caychem and his two had been gone for twenty-four hours. *Where were they?*

Rain beat harder on him, mixed with hail that stung him. Out in the storm, Conrad's voice carried, cursing mules, God, and the sky, over the drum and roar of the rain. Myra stood holding her reins and huddled close to Slocum. In all the misery of the storm, they both laughed at the mule skinner's defiance.

Then the storm passed. The sun soon twinkled on the diamonds that clung to the leaves of the wildflowers in purple and yellow and the heading grasses. Slocum went to join the skinners to help unload the mules. He had goose bumps on the back of his arms, and his saturated clothing stuck to his skin. He'd be glad when the sun's heat dried him out.

On the slopes above them, the pines looked fresh washed and the turpentine smell filled the air. Myra would need some poles to make the tent he promised her. After they off loaded, he'd take an ax and fell her some post-sized ones. Soon they were unloaded, assisted by the three scouts. The job complete, Slocum palavered with Tom about the absence of Caychem and the other two.

"You want me to go look for him?"

Slocum agreed. "He might need help."

"Silver Bar and Trigger can stay here. I'll go and see about them."

"Good."

So Tom set out on foot. Apaches liked to be in their moccasins a lot when they scouted. Slocum hoped that Tom learned something and nothing had happened to his other three men.

"I'm going to chop some poles," he told the others and took the double-bitted ax from Myra.

Then he and Roman set out for the hillside. They took turns felling and stripping off the branches with a hand ax. Soon the pile of useable ones began to stack up. Conrad brought a stout horse and roped them together in wads of three and four to drag them back. In a short while they had a pile in camp. She had the Apaches helping to spread out the new canvas sheets. In no time, the crew strung two tents up, twelve by twelve, that would protect them from the next rain.

Slocum checked the shoes on Strawberry and Myra's horse. They were nailed on secure and didn't need to be reset. He dropped Strawberry's back hoof in time to see his returning scouts with Tom trotting alongside their horses.

"I better get some food cooked," Myra said, wiping a curl of hair back with her hand. "They'll be hungry as vultures by this time."

"Right," Slocum agreed. He wondered what Caychem had learned about the ones on the trail. Early that day, they'd left Hernandez's wounded man Manuel on the trail. If someone came along, they might take him to where he could get medical aid. It was that or shoot him. Outlaws assumed their own risks in life. Live by the gun, die by it. Anyone else would have hung him for attempted horse thievery.

"Ho!" Caychem shouted when he drew up and nodded his approval at the tents.

"What did you learn?" Slocum asked, when he bounced off his horse and one of the other scouts took his bridle reins to lead it off.

"We had a fight with the one that Tom called Corallis this morning."

"Your men look all right. What happened?"

"They were planning to ambush you. Anyone after the girl, they planned to ambush."

Slocum nodded, waiting for the rest of the Apache's story.

"Three of his men are dead, but Corallis—he escaped and ran away."

"You did good. He will have to ride back to Fronteras to get more help."

Caychem nodded and grinned. "The girl is still alive."

"She's in Wolf's camp then?"

He bobbed his head and shifted his weight to his other leg as they squatted in the warming sun.

No need to ask an Apache how he knew anything. He knew. Amantha Grant was still alive. *Damn, that meant taking on the renegades and getting her out alive.* They simply had to somehow slip her out of their camp.

"How do we get her out?"

"Separate her from the others."

Slocum considered the answer. He looked around—everyone was there, but Myra, who was cooking from the smell of the wood smoke in the air. He nodded at them. They still had lots of work to do.

"We need an Apache on both ends of the canyon to be sure we aren't attacked here without warning for our guns and supplies." Everyone nodded. "That leaves four scouts and me to go get her."

Caychem nodded his approval. "We can catch them sleeping."

"Good, we don't need her shot up or hurt."

"Send Trigger down to get plenty creosote bush leaves," Caychem said. "We can rub ourselves with them and Wolf's dogs will not smell us."

"Good idea. Then we must do this at night?"

Tom nodded. "Bad time for Apaches, but also they will be asleep."

Slocum looked at the ground by his once fine boots, now scuffed and dusty. Only an Apache could do this. He better plan to stay at the edge of camp and let his men secure her. *Damn,*

where was Hernandez really at? Or any of the other bandits—
even Phillipe—he didn't trust them if they did get the girl. As
well as the renegade Apaches who'd sure want her back.

"When do we need to do all this?"

"Tonight, before they know we are here," Caychem said.

"All right. If we get split up, Roman, you and Conrad get
Myra back safely across the border. You scouts help them."

"Goddamn good cook, we not let anything happen to her," Silver Bar said.

They all laughed and agreed. Trigger asked if he should leave.

"Grab some of her damn good food," Slocum said, and they
laughed again.

Later when the men were fed, Slocum took her to the side.
"Sorry, this hasn't been nothing but work for you."

"Hey, I love these guys. I wasn't sure about the Apaches at
first, but hey, they flirt and act grateful for every bite I cook."

In the shadows of the tall ponderosa pines, she leaned her
back against the bark. "Do you think you're close to getting her?"

"I think we may get her tonight. But that will put us in the gun
sights of every two-bit bandit and outlaw in Mexico. If we do,
we'll split up. You, Jones, and Conrad plus the scouts will head
back for the border fast as you can get there. I plan to take her and
ride hard for there, but best that we go by separate ways."

"So," she said, leaning her head back against the tree. "This is
my last night with you—for awhile?"

"For awhile. I hope not very long."

"I hope not too." She unbuttoned her blouse, not looking up at
him. "Because I am going to need some attention." Her fingers
undid the ties on her skirt while her brown nipples dodged in and
out of his view in the open-front shirt. "So big man, you better
get your pants down." Wiggling, she slid the skirt off her hips.
"Because I intend to"—she peered around to be certain they were
alone—"screw you to death."

"Really?" he asked, toeing off his boot.

"As close to it as I can and not bury you."

"Good, but these pine needles—" He looked wryly at the
ground around them.

"I didn't lead you over here to get my backside all scuffed up
in that crap." She stepped over and unfurled her bedroll, conve-

niently stacked behind a tree. After she kicked a few twigs away, she unrolled it like a magic carpet across the forest litter. Sitting down, she fought off her boots and socks.

In the subdued light that shown through the dense overhead boughs and thick trunks, beams danced on her reddish-brown hair and reflected off her breasts that quaked when she moved.

Undressed and barefooted, he stepped onto her soft cotton top blanket and pulled her to him. Her rock-hard nipples pushed in his corded belly below the navel and her hot breath was on the lower part of his rib cage. He bent over and kissed the top of her head. Her small fingers played with his half-full dick and massaged his scrotum.

"When this is all over will you come live with me in the valley?"

"I wish I could. But we'd never be safe. Some bounty hunter would learn where I was at and there'd be shooting—killing—death." His fingers twined in her thick hair and he clutched her face to him as she nibbled on him.

"They'd never think you were a Mormon farmer."

"I've been everything else but that, and they still somehow learn my whereabouts. I've been around in that region too long. After this is over"—he sighed, enjoying her fingers' activity on his fast-growing erection—"I'll have to ride on."

She lowered herself and with half-closed evil eyes looked up, taking his manhood in her small fist. "Round one. I want to get the first round with you over like this, then you'll last longer on the next two."

He looked to the boughs above for some celestial help. Her hot mouth and lips closed on the swelling shaft. Like a hungry serpent, her tongue rubbed the upper side of the ring and his hips thrust his dick hard forward for all he could get in her mouth. Brain swirling, he gripped her head and pushed in and out hard. Sharp teeth raked on the head and sent lightning up his spine. His shortness of breath came on like a wind-broken horse and the muscles in his legs tightened. His efforts grew even more frenzied in the whirlpool suction of her mouth—then he threw his head back and came.

When he looked down, she was grinning up at him. The evidence like thick condensed milk ran from both corners of her mouth. She never lost her smirky gaze, dropping to the bedroll and pulling him after her. Her snowy short legs spread apart, the triangle of black pubic hair shown in the beams of the bloody sunset. The pink lips of her gates, glazed with moisture, were in contrast to the ivory skin that surrounded the portal. Her arms held out to receive him, she licked away the traces of evidence on her mouth.

In seconds, they were one. His hard sword fighting her swollen walls to reach the bottom. She cried aloud and pounded his arms with the sides of her fists. Slocum closed his eyes and thrust faster and harder. There was no one but him and her in the Sierra Madres—locked together in mortal battle.

8

The renegades' camp sat deep in the bowels of the mountains. Slocum wondered about all the owls' hooting. The nocturnal bird was a point of contention with the Apaches. They revered and feared it. Warriors would hear an owl hoot and refuse to go on the warpath—sometimes the birds spoke of death, sometimes forewarned of plagues like smallpox. Standing on the steep hillside in a grove of large pines, he wondered what they were speaking about. His four scouts, or Wolf's encampment of a half dozen wickiup that looked stark in the starlight.

He dried his hands on his britches. The wool pants were warm in the mountain air's coolness, but less than ideal for they snagged on everything he went past. A tough pair of canvas ones would have been better-suited for this trip though they usually galled him until they got softened by many washings and rainstorms. Sweating in the desert crossing had rubbed him raw on the inside of his legs when he wore.

Where was Caychem? He and two others had gone to search the camp for the girl. The rifle in his hands, Slocum studied the layout for any signs. The creosote must have worked; none of the camp dogs barked—if they had any. Indians could usually find some, even in remote places like the Madres.

Then he saw her being led by the hand from a wickiup. Her blond hair shone like silver in the starry night. Slocum raised his rifle and searched through the sights to cover anything that came out to threaten his men. They were soon beyond the perimeter and coming up the draw.

So far so good. Slocum kept his eyes on things for any movement as he began to hear the soft thread on the needles as they

48

ran uphill. When the sounds of her hard breathing grew loud enough in his ear, he eased the hammer down.

"Amantha?"

"Yes—" Her hair looked tangled and she wore a blanket kept shut by her hand.

"Your father sent us."

A dull nod.

"We have horses. I can carry you."

She shook her head and motioned for them to go ahead.

He gave the nod to his scouts. Caychem and the girl started up the hillside. The younger two Apaches covered their back tracks. Slocum kept his eye on her as she struggled on the slope ahead of him.

At last they were at the horses and she put her face on the saddle with a sigh. "I never believed anyone was ever coming."

"We're here and going to take you back. Can I help you get on?"

"Look the other way. I have no clothing, save this blanket."

"Sorry, I have a shirt in my saddlebags—" He searched around. *No time.* "You can put it on later."

She swallowed hard. "I would be grateful."

Mounted, they headed up the steep mountain in and out of the dark stands of tall pine where one could not see his hand in front of his face, then out in the pearl lighted openings in the timber.

The skin on Slocum's back crawled. Despite the fact that two scouts were covering their escape, he felt any minute there would be a scream or war cry and the hostiles would swarm on them like smoke out from the trees. They finally rode into a valley. Slocum reached in the saddlebags and handed her the shirt when they rested. Caychem went back and talked to his men.

"Thank you," she said quietly.

"No problem. Your father's been worried about you." The garment was three times too big and swallowed her, but she acted much more alert sitting up in the saddle than she had under the blanket.

"When he awoke me, I thought your man was one more Apache suitor who wanted my body."

"Sorry."

In the saddle with the blanket wrapped around her waist, she shook her head and then began to cry.

"I know," he said softly and patted her on the back. He looked back and saw no sign of Caychem or the others. "We've got to ride and ride and ride hard."

"I can do that," she said in a cracked voice.

"Let's go then."

They raced down the star-lighted valley southward. Spooking an occasional mule deer from his nocturnal grazing and a coatimundi family marching across the open made their horses shy. The long-nose raccoon family members fled the opposite way.

Slocum laughed and turned to her riding hard beside him.

She nodded in approval and looked elevated from her sorrow.

He hoped that when they were far enough away from the renegades' grasp she would return to what he thought she must have been, a fine young woman. Their horses' hooves beat a drum in the night.

At daybreak, they reached home camp. Their horses lathered and hot, Slocum gave the reins to Roman and told him to walk them. Then he helped her off the horse and steadied her.

"My gosh girl," Myra said in dismay at the sight of her. "I never thought you'd be alive."

"Myra, this is Amantha. She needs a skirt."

After the woman looked her over, she shrugged. "Mine might be a little short but I think I can find you one. I've got an old straw hat too. You really did sunburn your face."

"Oh, I'd be in your debt forever." She held the blanket around her waist and hurried after the shorter woman.

"I don't know about that." Myra looked around for him before she went among the packs. "Where are the others?" she asked Slocum.

"Setting a trap I guess for the renegades if they followed us."

"I see. Come on, honey. The dress shop's over in these panniers."

Satisfied that Amantha was in good hands, Slocum went to get some coffee.

"It beats all," Conrad said scratching his rumpled hair. "You getting her back right out from under them Apaches' noses."

Slocum squatted down, using his kerchief for a pot holder as he poured a tin cup full. "Want some?"

"Sure."

"Well, Apaches hate the night and they sleep hard unless on

the run. So they never suspected anyone was close by—given enough time and no signs, they figured any pursuit was over."

"You taking her back?"

"Yes. And the rest of you are taking Myra back."

"Gawdamighty, we sure won't let anything happen to her." Conrad shook his head, making a lock of hair fall in his face, and he swept it back. "That woman cooks like an angel. I'd gave up ever eating any real chow years ago. Army fart berries and sowbelly to grease your bowels. I've ate a million tons of that crap. Had the damn shits, day in day out. I'll be gawdamned, ain't had them one day on her cooking."

"Miracle."

"More than that."

Slocum blew on his coffee. Myra was bringing Amantha back wearing a riding skirt whose hem reached the middle of her shins. *No problem, she was dressed.*

"And finding that girl—Slocum, you are as slick as Tom Horn ever thought about being."

"I doubt that. Caychem and those two boys are the ones. But we aren't out of here yet." Slocum rose.

"When do you need to leave?" Myra asked him before she bent over to pour some coffee for Amantha.

"Soon. I'd like to be headed for the border in an hour."

"I have some jerky as well as corn meal and brown sugar packed in those small cloth bags." She gave a head toss at them and then handed Amantha a fresh cup full of strong coffee. "I hope it's enough food for the trip."

"We can find something I'm certain on the way."

"How many days to the border?" Myra asked. Amantha pushed up the floppy brim on her new hat and looked at him too for the answer.

"Three, if we can make it that fast."

"I'm sure ready," Amantha said, and they all nodded.

Slocum had Myra refill his cup.

"There's some beans and rice cooked," Myra said, "If you want to eat. Plenty of biscuits."

"Oh, that sounds heavenly," Amantha said and took a tin plate.

Slocum nodded in approval. He glanced back to the north. No sign of Caychem. He wished his scout would come on and give him a report about the movements of the renegades.

"You better take two fresh horses," Roman said, after walking the two to cool them out. "These two need some rest."

Slocum hated to leave Strawberry, but Roman was probably right. They'd pushed them hard for hours. Fresh horses would give them an edge. They'd need all of those advantages they could get. San Bernadino Springs—John Slaughter's ranch was his goal on the border.

The beans and rice were cooked in canned tomatoes, with chunks of fried sowbelly and some peppers. Along with Myra's biscuits, the food was filling, and he noticed Amantha even ate some. He hoped that lone wolf look on her face could be erased somehow—but he better worry more about getting her out of there and back in the U.S. than what the once beautiful girl would look like later.

Jones led up two fresh horses saddled for both of them.

"You be sure Myra gets back safe too," Slocum said, jamming his Winchester in the scabbard aboard the fresh horse Jones brought them.

"Hey, I ain't letting nothing happen to her. Hell, even old Conrad who hates women and all they stand for thinks she's a saint."

Slocum smiled and nodded. "Hard to get that old sum bitch to believe anything."

"Right," Jones said, holding the stirrup out for Amantha.

"Thank you," she said in a dry voice.

"No trouble, ma'am."

Slocum hurried over and hugged Myra. "You behave and listen to Jones. Him and Caychem will get you out of here. Once the two of us are gone, you should be less of a target."

"Be careful, big man. I know you're riding on. But by damn, when you come down the valley you better stop and see me."

"I will, and I'll have Roy Gene bring by your pay that Grant owes you."

"Good." She glanced down at her road-soiled clothing. "I could use a new change." Then she buried her firm breasts in his belly and hugged him tight. "Be careful."

"I will."

He could see the wetness gathering in her lashes. *Time to leave.* He kissed her on the mouth and then hurried for the bay horse. In the saddle, he nodded to his ward. She returned his head bob and they rode out of camp in a short lope.

Late afternoon, they reached a small village. Slocum knew the place as Blue Sky. Some goats raised up their heads and bleated at them. At their approach, a few yellow cur dogs barked as if an obligatory process.

"This a safe place?" Amantha asked.

"Safe enough to stop and eat some hot food. We won't stay here tonight."

She nodded.

He knew a woman who made good meals, and they reined up in front of her jacal. From inside he could hear someone cursing and at last the ample figure of Donna Montez appeared in the doorway. Her arms outstretched she ran out to hug him.

"Where have you been for so long, amigo?" She raised her brown eyes and blinked at the blond-haired girl still seated on her horse.

"You've got a woman?"

Slocum shook his head. "No, I am taking her home. Apaches brought her down here."

"Oh, my God," Donna cried and rushed over to help her down, talking in a low, reassuring voice. Mother-like, she guided his ward inside the jacal. Then she shouted for him to follow and went back to talking to Amantha in a soothing tone.

With both of them seated on a blanket spread over the hard packed floor, Donna nodded at him. "You always have nice lady friends. I must go out and fix you some food."

"Thanks," he said, drinking some of the red wine she'd poured for the two of them. In Mexico, he could usually trust the women. Most of the men were too greedy to mess with.

Amantha smiled at him when they were alone. Not a big wide one, but her tight lips turned up in the corners. "So my father hired you?"

"Yes, and then he put out a reward that made every pistolero in Mexico anxious to find you."

"Sounds like my father."

"He made things a lot harder than they would have been."

"You speak of running for the border?"

'We will. We're only a day or a day and a half away from the San Bernadino Ranch of John Slaughter. Once we get there, we can rest up and then ride on to your father's ranch."

"What lies ahead of us?"

"Desert mainly. You making it all right?"

"Yes." She swallowed hard and nodded. "I'll be fine."

"Would it help to cry?"

Her blond hair danced on her shoulders when she shook her head. "That can come later when we are at this ranch you speak about."

"Here we have some food," Donna said, breaking into the room from the outside with two trays of her rich-smelling Mexican dishes and tortillas.

"I could never eat that much," Amantha said, surveying her platter.

"Eat what you can. My food will heal you," Donna bragged.

"Listen to her," Slocum said, touching her arm. "Listen, Donna is a *bruja*."

The woman made a disapproving face at him. "Ignore Slocum. He doesn't know anything."

"I know witches, and you're one. A good fortune teller maybe, a wonderful cook, but still a *bruja*."

"The food tastes wonderful."

"Thank you, my dear, I may have to fix this big gringo. Calling me a witch. *Eawahlow*, hombre."

Slocum laughed as he swept up a tortilla to use as a food scoop. "Witches are witches."

After they finished eating, he thanked Donna and paid her.

"You must leave so soon?"

"Yes, we have many miles to cross. I fear there are bad men on our back trail."

Donna nodded gravely as if she knew, too, his concern anyway. "I will burn candles for your safe journey, *mi amigo*."

Then she hugged the girl tight like a mother. "You are lucky to have such a strong man to take you back home. Here, wear this straw hat—that one is too old for a pretty girl." She put the better straw sombrero on her, then bobbed her head in approval.

Amantha nodded in gratitude to her.

"You hombre, come by and visit and I will fatten you." Then she laughed aloud.

Their horses had finished the grain he bought for them. He tightened the cinches and helped his ward aboard. A tip of his hat and they rode off in the star-specked night. He rode in the saddle, twisted, and looked to the south—but he saw nothing in the inky night.

"How far will we ride?" she asked. "Oh, this hat is much better." She drew up the chin string and nodded at him.

"Good. We need to go a ways. I want some distance from there. There are always wagging tongues that will tell anyone we were there. Not hers, you understand, but others?"

"I see."

He made the horses trot. They crossed the greasewood plains with the saw-topped mountains on both sides as low silhouettes. Near midnight he halted them in a deep dry wash, offered her a blanket, and hobbled the animals.

"We can sleep here a few hours and let the horses rest, too. But if you hear anything, wake me if I am asleep."

"I will," she agreed.

The day's heat fast evaporated and the blanket felt good with the warmth of the sand radiating up from the bottom side. He fell asleep in minutes, after seeing her in a fetal position a few feet away.

"Horses coming," she hissed in his ear.

"Get to their muzzles and don't let them nicker to them." He threw back the covers, hearing the drum of many hooves drawing closer. Maybe in the dry wash they might go unseen in the starlight. No one without a light could track them at night. He held the bay by the nose and suppressed any sound from him. She did the same to her mount.

The hoofbeats grew louder and the creak of saddle leather too, as several riders came down the steep bank in a stiff-legged fashion on their hard-breathing horses. Even the strong smell of horse sweat carried to Slocum's nose. The riders were Mexicans by the outline of their sombreros, not Apaches; they cursed in Spanish and beat their tired mounts on northward.

Until their hoofbeats died away in the darkness, Slocum and the girl stood by their mounts. Then they dared to begin breathing again.

"Oh," she said and collapsed against him. "What will we do?"

Holding her in his arms, he looked after the pursuers' faint images fleeing north across the sagebrush sea in the pearly light.

"Change our directions some. If we head north we'll ride into them."

"But—" She felt limp in his arms, he was forced to bend over and scoop her up. He carried her over to the blankets and gently laid her down.

"You all right?"

"Sorry, I have never—fainted before." She sat up and moved the loose hair from her face.

"You're lucky. Take your time. We have some time."

"Where will we go if they are blocking the way?"

"Around them."

"Will that work?"

"It has to." Her words rung in his ears. No telling how many more bands of outlaws were out there looking for the two of them. He could only hoped that Myra, his scouts, and mule skinners were safe. *Damn Grant for offering such a large reward for her anyway.*

9

Day found them close to the foothills. He'd pushed the horses hard, wanting as much distance as possible. They found an abandoned *rancheria*. Many such operations had to be abandoned because of the fierce attacks of the roaming Apaches going back and forth from Arizona to the Sierra Madres.

"Anyone live here?" she asked.

"No. Not unless they're squatters."

"Will they find us here?" She twisted in the saddle and looked over their back trail. Then, as if satisfied, she turned back. "Who owns it?"

"Probably some rich *patron* in Mexico City. Apaches made it too hard on them out here so they abandoned these ranches. And so they have never been taken up again."

They dismounted and she studied the date palms and the plastered walls. "It looks fine."

"Good enough for us for few days," Slocum said, swinging a leg over and stepping off his horse. "Let me look around. Stay on your horse."

"Certainly." She took his reins as he loosened the Colt in the holster on his hip and slipped into the yard.

Dry weeds before the door were the only thing that made the place look deserted. His gaze was upon the tile floor when he entered the living area. No tracks in the dust, save some small animals. There was still furniture they'd left behind. Tables and chairs. He checked the courtyard. The fountain was dry, of course, but the perennial flowering vines looked half alive. Nothing out of place that he could see. They had either been killed or simply rode away. No sign of either. The place, he surmised, had

57

been empty for a long time, but yet looked very habitable.

He went back out and nodded to her. "It will do."

"How long will we stay here?"

"A day or so. Confuse them I hope when they don't find us up north."

She dropped heavily from the saddle. He went and undid the cinches while she looked around the outside.

"Go inside and rest, you look beat."

With a nod, she agreed and disappeared in the front way. He led the horses around to the pens. He found a pail and drew water from a well. The water had no bad smell or taste, so he poured it in a trough. The horses drank it quicker than he could keep up for awhile. Soon he began to get ahead of them by hand over hand pulling up the pail.

She joined him. "Where did the last ones to live here go?"

"They must have abandoned this place when the Apaches became so fearsome. There's several ranches like this between here and the border that were in their path and were either burned out or left."

"Could I take a bath in that?" She indicated the tank.

"Sure, but—"

"That's fine. A bath sounds wonderful. I haven't had one in so long I smell and feel rotten."

"There's some soap in my saddlebags. Wait, I'll get it, I need to unsaddle them and let those ponies roll."

"Wonderful," she said.

Her face was peeling and looked close to bleeding in places. Loose skin was sticking out, but under it the handsome looks of a young woman appeared. Tall and slender, even with her trail-dusted clothing, she carried herself light-footed and looked ready to dance away. Her blond hair despite a million twists and tangles still shone like gold in the sunlight. Amantha Grant was a very attractive girl of perhaps eighteen or so.

He tossed the saddles on the fence as she waited. Their feet set apart, the grateful ponies shook hard when he removed the kac. Then they began to lower themselves to the ground for a roll to scratch their itching backs. Four hooves in the air they wiggled on their spines enough to draw a smile on her lips.

"They're as happy as I will be after I bathe."

"Bath water coming up." He handed her the soap and the sack towel.

"But how will you—"

"That towel will dry in ten minutes. You won't hurt it. Go ahead."

She nodded. "I don't even know you very well, yet I owe my life to you."

"Not much to know. I'm the man your father hired to find you."

"And then he put out a reward?"

"Yes, after he hired me. I guess he was desperate." He began to pull up more water for her bath.

She looked off at the saw-edged, purple mountains. "I imagine my not coming home as planned did upset him. My father likes things to go as he plans them."

Slocum agreed. "Like trying to spook off all the landholders in Sulfur Springs Valley, especially the widows."

"I suppose that, too. What do you do when you aren't playing knight?"

He laughed at her and shook his head, pulling up another container of cool water.

"I play cards, and have a sugar foot."

"You mean you roam a lot."

"Yes." He hauled up another and dumped it. "That might have to sun heat a while."

Resolved, she shook her head. "I don't care. I want to rid myself of the smell."

"Suit yourself."

"You say you wander. Men are so lucky. If I was a son instead of daughter, I would go see the far ends of the earth. But that's not ladylike. Of course, my weeks with the Apache may have soiled my reputation so badly, no man will ever want me."

"Pretty as you are. . . ." Slocum grinned tight lipped. "Ain't much worries about that ever happening."

"You have embarrassed me."

"Why?"

"I don't consider myself pretty."

"Good, means you aren't conceited. I'll go up to the house and try to figure out what we can eat."

"Is there food left?"

"No, but that'll be an excuse so you can take a bath by yourself."

She chewed on her lower lip. "You could sit down with your back turned, and we could talk. I have missed conversing with people who speak English."

"Your call."

"Good," she said, undoing the buttons on the front of the shirt he'd loaned her.

He squatted down on his boot heels and faced away. It was hard for him not to turn and look when she let out a small scream. He knew the the water would be icy cold.

"Were you coming back from school?"

"Yes. St. Louis. Louise Turner's School of Charm. Where they tried to make me a lady, I guess."

"They did well."

"I was even engaged to Charles Rambolt, the third."

"Still are?"

She didn't answer him at first, only the sounds of her splashing. Then at last she spoke, "No, I plan to wire him and tell him it's all off."

"Why?"

"Who wants an Apache-soiled bride?"

"Maybe Charles does?"

"I won't live the rest of my life under a roof where that was held over me."

"You think he'd do that?"

"I'm sorry you can't see my head nod. Yes, I do."

"Then he wasn't the one to marry anyhow." He studied the small tracks in the dust made by some kangaroo rat.

"Perhaps you're right. Slocum . . . I'm sorry, but would you get a blanket for me to wear. These clothes are too filthy to put back on like they are."

"No trouble." He rose and started for the saddles.

"Don't worry about looking. Every Apache buck in the land has seen me naked."

Slocum undid the bedroll, pulled out a blanket. Going back, he eyed her willowy ivory figure standing beside the trough, hugging herself from the coldness that rapid evaporation caused. He fit it over her shoulders and she looked at him with her eyes the color of the azure sky. "Thanks."

"I need to go find us some supper."

"What?"

"A deer or jackrabbit."

"Big difference," she said.

"Yes, about the amount of meat on them there is."

They both laughed uneasily, standing only a few feet apart. He knew if he didn't cut out right then this casual affair at arm's length would grow tougher.

"I'll be back," he said to assure her and turned on his heels.

"I'm counting on it," she said softly after him.

He took the Winchester. Since the place had not been occupied for such a long time, finding a deer or any game close by might not be too hard. He found a dry wash and walking its bank could see the traces of a small spring in the green mossy ribbon in the middle of the sand. A few yards further he noticed the tops of a few cottonwoods tucked in the waterway. Cottonwoods and water usually meant game.

In a steady stealth, he moved bent low down, back far enough from the rim to get close and yet be unseen. In a few minutes, he was even with the trees and could hear all the birds, especially the small Sonoran doves cooing. Then he spotted something yellow. A buckskin color. Three of them were standing broadside to him. The smaller Mexican desert pronghorn antelope. The rifle butt pressed to his shoulder, he squared the iron sights on the chest of the middle one and squeezed.

His intended jumped high in the air, hit hard. They whirled in a blur and were gone. Slocum dropped on his haunches and waited. The antelope was shot in a fatal spot and would not go far if not spooked. The birds began to sing again as if nothing had happened. Though he could not see his game, he knew it had not gone far.

After fifteen minutes, he found a way off the bluff and crossed the wash. Several were from horses and cattle that had recently used the water hole. No doubt they were long gone wild abandoned livestock. He found the carcass a hundred yards from where he shot it.

The young buck weighted perhaps fifty pounds. A miniature of the ones on the great plains even when full size. Slocum drug him back to the water hole to dress and wash him out. There he hung him over a limb by putting a green stick through his lower leg tendons. Then, careful to keep split hair off the meat, he inserted his skinning knife's sharp point and began to open the body using the blade on the underside of the skin. Soon the guts were spilled out. Ordinarily he'd have saved the liver, but this time he was anxious to get the job completed and get back as the sun hung low in the west.

The copper smell of entrails in his nose, his bloody fingers stiffened as they dried. Soon the guts were removed and the skinning began in earnest. With care, he soon had the hide off the fat carcass and washed it in the spring. Knife and hands clean, he shouldered his meat, picked up his rifle and headed back. There would be lots of good eating and they could jerk the rest if they had the time. His mouth watered for some juicy loin, slow cooked over a mesquite fire.

When he came in sight, she was standing on her toes searching for him, dressed in her cleaner-looking still damp clothes. Her gold hair sparkled and hung in long curls—obviously she had brushed it.

"Did you give up on me?" he asked.

"No. My, you did get a deer."

"No, an antelope."

"Well, it looks good anyway."

"Young and fat. That's what matters."

She fell in beside him. "I heard the shot a long time ago."

"Takes time."

"I guess I was impatient for your return."

"We both will be before we get him cooked."

"No." She shook her head and looked at the sky bleeding with sundown. "We'll be better to be close to each other."

Slocum agreed. "But we need to gather up some firewood or we won't ever get him cooked."

"I have some gathered. That's what I've done since you left."

He smiled at her. "Good girl."

"You learn about such things in training to be a squaw. Wood or fuel was the first thing you sought when you made camp."

Slocum chuckled. "I was dreading doing that."

"No, woman's work," she said with an Apache accent.

With his rifle-holding hand, he hugged her shoulders. "This is going to fun."

"I hope so."

Watching the sunset gather in a fiery ball in the west, he really hoped their time spent together was all fun.

The fire burned down onto hot coals under the grate in the fireplace; he put on the loins and one back ham. The rest they would jerk in the morning, if time allowed. Seated cross-legged side by side on the tile floor and the fire's heat reflection in their face, the strong aroma of the burning desert woods filled his nose.

She reached over and put his arm on her shoulder, then scooted closer until her head rested on his chest. "Hold me?"

He hugged her. And wished he had taken a bath, but for the moment he wanted to savor his time with her. The closeness of her subtle body to him settled his mind from racing over the details of outdoing an enemy in pursuit—somewhere out there in the night. Were Myra and the others safely back to the border? They should be.

Then he looked down and their gaze met. He used his forefinger to raise her chin and then he kissed her. Her arms snaked around his neck as two forces went head on. Mouth to mouth, he found the hunger inside her wasn't for food alone. His tongue searched her mouth and she clung to him harder. Soon she sat upon his lap to get more of him.

His hand molded the teacup-sized hard breast under the shirt. In seconds she fumbled with the buttons and soon pushed his calloused palm under the cloth. When he cupped it, she sucked in her breath. He smiled and they began to kiss again—this time even more demanding. A world of headiness swirled around them until at last out of breath he tore his mouth away.

Her cradled in his arms, he rose.

"The meat will burn?"

He shook his head looking down at her.

"There's a bed in there," she said. "No mattress—"

He cut off her words with his lips. She clutched him tight and returned the fury.

The pearl-lighted room held a bedstead where she had rolled out their bedding. He set her on the edge and she began to unbutton her skirt and blouse. He toed off his boots and then took off his vest and shirt. When he unbuckled his gun belt she moved in.

Quickly she undid the belt buckle and then the buttons and

jerked down his pants. Flush faced she looked up at him. "I wanted to do this since I first saw you. I'm not repulsive, am I?"

He pulled her up and hugged her tight. "My God, no, girl. You have me trembling to get to you."

"Great," she said as if relieved and pulled him on the bed after her. Fumbling around, they fought him free of his underwear. With only their blankets on the board frame, it was firm under his knees when he waded over her snowily slender legs to get between them.

For a quick second, he made himself a picture of her firm teacup-sized breasts capped by pink nipples. Her slender form down to the bare pubic area with only the least amount of peach fuzz coating a triangle. Her eyelids closed she raised her hips for his entry. He eased the turgid nose in her gates and she yelled out when he entered her ring.

"Oh!" she cried, arching her back for more.

Probing into her gently, he braced himself above her and his hips ached to thrust deeper and deeper. Her small fingers closed on his forearms and she began to rock underneath him. Legs wrapped around him, her bare heels spurred him on. The effort grew stronger. Soon her walls began to expand, pulling harder and harder on his about-to-burst sword.

Mouth open, out of breath, she tossed her head in pleasure and ecstasy beneath him. His drive grew faster and faster. She was pounding the back of her head on the bed with a soft, "Yes," at every plunge. Their rhythm grew wilder. His breath raged through his throat and his ears rang. Then some unseen hand squeezed both his testicles. Two burning needles struck deep in his buttocks and relief exploded inside her in one great effort that drew his strength with it.

Dazed and shaken, they lay side by side in the darkness.

"Oh, the meat will burn," she said, bolting up, holding his shirt to cover her nakedness.

He smiled as she clambered over him, her silky skin tracing over his bare legs. *Who needs food?* He closed his eyes and laid his head back down.

"It's all right," she hissed from the door like no one else was to hear.

"Good," he said, ready to sleep.

"Aren't you going to eat?"

"I reckon I better," he said, at last throwing his legs over the edge, scrubbing his bearded face and wishing he could sleep for a week.

10

"I could stay here forever with you," she said, looking back at the casa.

"We'd never get anything done." He grinned as she swirled around in the bright sun like a ballerina with her straw hat on her outstretched arm.

She threw her sombrero in the air as if to toss it all away. "Who would care?"

He used his calloused hand to run over his clean-shaven chin. He damn sure didn't care either. But until she was back home, Grant's reward hung over her pretty head as a threat to her safety. Finally washed and cleaned up, he felt depleted by their furious and frequent lovemaking. Time to move on. They needed to make it to the San Bernadino Ranch in the next two days. And somehow avoid Hernandez's men while getting back to the U.S.A. Once there, he might even have trouble getting across the Sulfur Valley—damn her father and his stupid reward.

An hour later with fresh horses underneath them, they short loped northward.

"You don't think those men that passed us are waiting?"

"We are on another course right now. They never tracked us to the ranch."

"So you think it's safe?"

"Love, I don't think anything's safe until you're home."

She wrinkled her nose at him. "I think going there is like going to prison."

"He's not my father."

"No, he's mine, but he's so hardheaded."

They plied their mounts off a loose bank into a dry wash,

66

struck the bottom, and raced on. Until noon he was holding their speed down to a trot to save the animals. Soon some green appeared. The tops of some cottonwoods shown in the distance. They approached an outpost called Louie's. Slocum expected this to be a place for him to be cautious, but doubted the pistoleros were there.

"Is this going to be safe?" she asked, twisting in the saddle as they walked to cool their mounts.

"Safe enough, I hope."

"Why do we stop here then?"

"The horses need water. We may have to camp tonight in the desert so we better water them when we can."

"I see."

"In case anything happens, don't look back—ride as hard as you can straight north. John Slaughter will see that you get safely home."

"What about you?"

"You heard me."

"Yes, sir."

"Well, listen. If they get both of us, then no one is well off. At least if you get away—you'll make it home."

She wrinkled her peeling nose at him. "I won't like leaving you."

"You know, you ever heal from that sun burning you'd make a right pretty gal." Then he laughed big at her as they walked along. "Not half bad."

Her face red, she stepped over with a menacing fist. "I ought to hit you."

"Oh, please don't—"

"You're a mess—well, anyway."

At the small village's well and trough, after looking over things, Slocum dismounted with a jingle of his spurs. Birds chirped in the dollar-sized pale leaves fluttering overhead. A young boy watered three goats and ducked his head bashfully.

Slocum's hand never left the butt of his .44. He constantly scanned the jacals and the fallen in building with the faded letters on the front above the tattered palm frond-covered porch. LOUIE'S. Nothing looked out of place. No sign of a bandit's hat or a good horse and saddle. He handed her the canteens to refill—unable to shake the wary feelings in his gut about the possible danger lurking unseen. Every muscle in his body tensed for action.

"Been any pistoleros around here?" Slocum asked the goat boy.

"Not today."

"Yesterday?"

"A few. They rode south."

Slocum tossed him a ten centavo coin and the boy's brown eyes flew open like saucers looking at it in his brown palm. *"Gracias, gracias."*

Then he drug away his resistant goats that each wanted to go in different directions. The canteens filled, Slocum swung in the saddle, still not satisfied, but grateful to be on the move again. He dried his sweaty gun hand on his pants leg and told her they needed to lope.

"Why—"

His hard look froze off her words and they headed north. The dusty wagon tracks dropped off into a wide wash, sliced by a small trickle of water. Slocum saw the man when he stepped out from behind a cottonwood tree with a rifle at his shoulder. Slocum's hand went to his gun butt. The Colt in his fist spoke and caused his horse to shy sideways. His second shot found a mark and the man went down, his rifle going off in the dust. Slocum turned to her. "Ride north and hard!"

For a moment, she started to rein up, but he reached over and lashed her horse on the butt.

"Go! I'm coming behind you."

She looked back at him as if hurt, then went to spurring and slapping her own horse to go faster. Slocum swung his horse around, looking for any more threat. No movement. Was the man facedown on the ground alone? He doubted it.

In long minutes, he saw her reach the ridge. No more threats, he fled after her, holstering the Colt as he went. In a few minutes, he was on her trail as she sent a cloud of dust from her horse's heels bearing between the low greasewoods along the road.

Beside her at last, he indicted for her to slow down. Nothing on their back trail, he didn't want their horses run into the ground. It was still over forty miles to Slaughter's.

"Who was he?"

"Damned if I know, but they left him there to shoot me, I'm satisfied, figuring you would be easy to pick up if I was gone."

"Not very easy." Indignation shone on her face.

"Without water and a long ways from a place that was safe, they'd run you down out here."

"What do we do now?"

"Ride all night. Slaughter's is the only place that I figure is safe."

"You know him?"

"Have for years. We use to stop off there on our way into and out of Mexico when I was with the army chasing Apaches down here. Tough little man."

"I've never met him."

"His wife Buffie is nice, too." Slocum twisted in the saddle. No sign of a dust plume against the azure sky to indicate pursuit. Still he felt uneasy. They'd be better off at the ranch.

"We need to trot."

She agreed and they rode north. The reflected heat seared his face and dried his eyes until they felt loaded with grit looking across the dull gray land before them.

Why leave one gunman? That meant something. Maybe this Hernandez had men all across northern Sonora in a line to stop him since they'd lost his trail. No telling—he only wished he had some better information on what lay ahead for them.

"Let's lope."

By sundown, he began to see sign's of Slaughter's operation. They rode past the empty working pens and watered their horses at the huge rock-mortar tank and windmill, spooking off some roan–longhorn cross cows and calves.

Amantha scrubbed her face in the warm, mossy water. No matter, the liquid refreshed both of them. He used his kerchief for a washcloth and finally soaked his head under the surface, seeking some escape from the broiling heat in his skin.

She collapsed on her butt finally, looking relieved but beat. "How much further?"

"Six to eight hours."

"These his pens?"

"Yeah, but he owns half of Arizona and half of Sonora."

She laughed and struggled to her feet. "I hope he has a bed."

"He will."

"I may sleep for two days."

"You need that long, he'll let you."

"Don't you have a home? A wife somewhere? A family?"

He shook his head. "A long time ago up in Kansas, a half-drunk boy came back to a bar after losing in a card game to shoot me. I shot him instead. The law up there called it murder. His father owns the law."

"How long ago was that?"

"Years."

"So you're still on the run?"

"Yes." He checked her cinch. "We better ride."

"I'm sorry I asked. Guess I was being selfish and if you weren't taken I wanted you."

"You flattered me."

"No—" She shook her head, mounting her horse. Reins gathered, she looked down and knowingly smiled at him. "I'm not the first woman that ever wanted you, and I suspect I won't be the last."

He mounted and gave her a nod. She was right. He hoped so anyhow—'cause when she was safely back home, he'd have to ride on. They rode off in the dwindling light.

Hours later, they began to pass dark jacals, barking dogs, and irrigated fields in the starlight. Slocum began to relax in the saddle. At last, the row of tall cottonwoods stood out like giant ghost forms on the horizon as they rode up to he silver pool fed by the San Bernadino Springs. The forms of the house, the ranch store, and buildings to the west looked dark.

"We don't need to wake them," he said, "We can throw our blankets down right here."

"Good," she said and dismounted. "Hobble him?"

"No, he won't leave the grass and water here."

"This is what they call an oasis, isn't it?"

"Yes." He stripped the saddles off and piled them on the ground and went to help her spread the blankets.

"It is so beautiful."

He agreed. Quickly, she spread out their bedroll and on her knees in the center of it she waited for him.

"Will you hold me tight?"

"Tight as you want."

"Oh, I wanted one more night of that—" She raised the hair off her neck to let the cooling night wind sweep over her skin.

He toed off his boots. "I assure you that's about all I can do."

"No problem—my eyelids are so heavy—"

11

John Slaughter was a short man with a pointed goatee. In knee-high English riding boots, tweed pants, and vest, he looked more like an English lord than a rancher. He sat a large black horse and clung to the saddle horn with both hands, shaking his head as if amused.

"I have trespassers, I see."

Slocum raised up to a sitting position in the bedroll and combed his hair back through his fingers. "Bad ones too. We got here kinda late and figured you'd be grouchy as a sore-toed bear getting up for the two of us."

"Slocum. I wondered if that was you. And the lady?"

"Another man's wife."

"I am not!" Amantha squinted at Slaughter against the golden rays of sunlight coming up in the east and shook her head.

"Amantha Grant," Slocum said and yawned open-mouthed.

"Oh," Slaughter said, dropping off his horse. "The one the big reward is being offered for."

"That's the one."

"Well, you two better come to the house. Buffie has breakfast ready or will in a short while, and she loves company."

"Good," Amantha said, threw the covers back and stood up.

"You two must be ducking trouble to come this way," Slaughter said.

"Everyone in Mexico wants the reward." Slocum put on his hat and stood up.

She was already rolling up the blankets. "You must know my father."

"Yes, I've meet him at some stockman meetings."

"He's hardheaded and going to get his way."

71

"Looks like he'll soon get his daughter back."

Bent over tying the bedroll, she craned her head around to look at him. "But not for long."

Slaughter chuckled. "Come by the house you two."

"We will," Slocum promised as he watched Slaughter mount up and ride for the headquarters.

"Saddle up?" she asked.

"No, we can walk over there. We're safe here, and my butt's sore enough from all that riding."

"I'm too filthy to go in her house."

"Slaughter's wife Buffie won't mind. She's a lot younger than he is."

"Oh."

"His first wife died on a stage coming to Arizona several years back. He married Buffie, hardly more than a girl then, and she raised his two children."

What Slocum promised came to forte. Buffie hugged her and found her a real hairbrush and had a Mexican woman draw her a bath after breakfast. They gathered her clothing and took them off to be washed. She also promised Amantha a new set of clothes that would fit her.

Slocum and Slaughter drank whiskey in the shade of the front porch and talked about old times. His dusty, run-over boots propped up on the rail, Slocum leaned back and listened to Slaughter's talking about renegade Apaches slow elking his beef and making a nuisance of themselves.

"I'd give them the damn beef. I just hate one that's wasted. They sometimes only cut a leg off or take only the loin."

"Guess that's how they eat?"

Slaughter nodded. "They do have a pretty tough time living in a past century. You taking her home?"

"I guess in the morning we'll start north."

"Better ride up the San Pedro side of the Chiricuhuas."

Slocum blinked at his host and dropped his boots to the wooden porch flooring. "You know something I don't?"

Leaned back, glass in hand, Slaughter pulled on his goatee, then nodded. "My guess is her father doesn't intend to pay you that reward."

"Whew, thanks. I bet his men are back to harassing the Mormon women in the valley over there too."

With a slight bob of his head and a grim set to his mouth, Slaughter answered him. "Grant's not too valuable an asset to the territory in my book."

"He may be even be less—dead," Slocum said, looking at the dust of some riders coming in.

"I agree. You get some time and need some work, I'd pay you well to gather a force and eliminate my Apache problem."

Pained, Slocum shook his head. "Not the job for me."

Slaughter stood up and looked at the line of distant riders. "Wouldn't be fun. Tom Horn told me the same thing, not six months ago. Damn it, they remain a real problem. Even after the daring raid when they took her and killed several more, the U.S. Army still won't do anything. Like the whole fucking business is over for them."

"Send Geronimo to Florida and that ended it, huh?"

"Right, but they're still raiding out of the Madres."

"If you don't pay them any mind, maybe they'll go away." Slocum grinned at him.

Slaughter shook his head, rose, and stood by the porch post. "You know these men coming here?"

"They might work for a guy called Hernandez." Slocum noticed the peak-crowned sombreros on their heads.

"Never heard of him."

Slocum rose and stepped to put his shoulder to the other porch post. "He ain't worth much."

"*Buenos dias*, senor," the lead rider on a big gray horse said and removed his sombrero.

"Good day. What can I do for you?" Slaughter asked.

"Surrender the woman he brought here and you will have no trouble, senor." The man indicated Slocum.

"You hombres been out in the sun too long. Right now there's a double barrel-shotgun and two Winchesters pointed at your hearts. Did you come here to die?"

When the riders turned, Slocum saw the man appear on the roof of the shed with a rifle butt on his shoulder and looking down the iron sights at them. From the corner of the house, a black man appeared with a double Greener ready in his hands. That was John T, Slaughter's man, some say an ex slave who stayed, others said he was his own son. No doubt the seriousness of their situation had reached the five men on horseback.

"My mistake, senor," the man said with a bow and replaced his hat. "With your permission we shall leave."

"Hold up. What's your name?" Slaughter demanded.

"Pacho, Pacho Alverez."

Slaughter shot a questioning look at Slocum, who shook his head.

"You work for an hombre called Hernandez?" Slaughter demanded.

"*Si*, senor."

"You tell that border riffraff of a boss of yours, if he or any of you harms my friend here or that girl, I'll search you out and gut shoot all of you. Hear me?"

"*Si*."

"It's a tough way to die. Now get the hell off my ranch."

They needed no more encouragement and fled southward in a cloud of dust.

"John T., you recognize any of them?" Slaughter asked his black servant.

"Na, sah, but I bets they don't come back." The black man cracked open the Greener and removed the tall copper cartridges. He pocketed them, then snapped the gun shut. "I knows what they look like now. They comes around again I shoot first and ask them questions 'fore they's die."

"Good." Slaughter gave a sigh and indicated the chairs. "Ride up the San Pedro Valley."

"I believe you're right," Slocum said, retaking his seat. "Thanks, sorry I brought them on you."

"No trouble. Those kind need killed on sight."

Slocum sat back down and considered his half-full glass. *They probably did.*

Amantha emerged with John's elegant wife Buffie on the porch. Dressed in a well-fitted divided riding skirt and long-sleeved blouse, she looked very fresh with her blond hair hair brushed to a sheen. Her face looked tanned and the remnants of her peeling were gone.

"You look absolutely gorgeous," Slaughter said.

Slocum agreed.

"Who was here?" Buffie asked.

"Some border scum. We sent them packing."

Buffie nodded as if satisfied.

SLOCUM AND THE SULFUR VALLEY WIDOWS   75

"I plan to leave here after dark," Slocum said to Amantha. "Will you be rested enough?"

"Yes, I'll be fine."

"And I'm loaning you some fast horses," Slaughter added.

Slocum nodded in approval. "Thanks, we can use them."

"My father will repay you."

"They are a gift to you, my dear."

Amantha fought blushing, but the red highlighted her cheeks. "Thank you, very much."

"Now, Slocum and I can get back to telling each other interesting lies." He toasted them with his glass.

"I imagine you will be glad to get home, won't you my dear?" Buffie asked, leading her off.

Amantha gave Slocum a last look over her shoulder as the woman herded her off into the house.

The glance was enough. He decided Amantha at the moment dreaded the homecoming worse than Apaches or bandits. But the inevitable was at hand; if they pushed fresh horses all night, they'd be a Grant's in the midmorning. She had to go home.

They left the San Bernadino Springs by starlight. Buffie motherly hugged her and kissed Slocum on the cheek.

"Come back, both of you, when this is over."

"I can't thank you enough," Amantha said.

"Oh darling, it was fun having you here," Buffie said.

"Yes, it was. I didn't have to listen to all the things I need to do while you were here," Slaughter said, removing his hat and bowing to her.

Amantha ran over and kissed the short man on the forehead. "Thanks, anyway."

They short loped northward. The towering giant range of mountains on their left and the sun-cured, grassy valley looked snowy white in the night. A wide plains that fled northward as they rode hard.

By sunup, they were north of the Chiricuhuas high peaks and soon rounded them, headed westward. They struck the Southern Pacific tracks before noon and rode on to the Wilcox station. Paused to eat some fried chicken that Buffie sent along: they washed down the tasty meal with tepid canteen water. The horses rested hip shot under a cottonwood in a dry wash.

Midafternoon, they reached the ranch and rode up the two ruts cut in the grass that formed the road in. Neither had said much during the ride. Slocum felt a curtain being pulled between them. Like she wanted to withdraw from him. If that made it easier for her to return home, then so be it.

"You still look nice," he said to reassure her.

"Nice enough to go to work in some cathouse?"

He frowned at her.

"I am soiled. I guess the entire territory, even the nation, knows that by now."

"I guess you could go on feeling sorry for yourself the rest of your life too."

She nodded. "I guess I could. I will try not to."

"Good. You're a worthy person. Any man gets you will be lucky."

"We'll see."

"Why is that?"

"Charles Rambolt, the third, was coming out here to ask my father for my hand and to propose. I suspect he'll conveniently not come."

"He'd be a damn fool if he doesn't come out here."

"He's that all right." She looked off across the plateaus of water that shimmered under the sun.

"I wish you the best of luck."

"I'd live in a hovel in Mexico with you."

"It would get old." He wrinkled his nose at her.

"You don't think living in a mansion for a prison isn't boring?"

He had no answer for her.

When they rode up to the house, Grant came out on the porch smoking a cigar.

"You found her, did you? Hello, Amantha."

"Hello, Father." She slipped off the big bay and gave Slocum the reins.

"Come inside, I'll pay you."

Slocum shook his head. "I'll wait out here."

Twisted in the saddle, he saw no sign of any of Grant's gun hands and turned back to look at the man.

"Have it your way. Go in the house, my dear."

"I'll wait out here until you pay him," she said.

Grant blinked as if displeased with both of them. Then he stomped off into the house, mumbling to himself.

"Be careful," she said in a quiet voice.

He checked around again. "Maybe you better go inside when he comes out."

"Why?"

"I intend to give him a piece of my mind."

"I'd love to hear it—but I'll go in."

Grant strode out and handed Slocum a bag of money. He put it in his saddle bags and turned back. He watched her go inside before he spoke. "We made a deal. You were to leave those women in the valley alone."

"Yeah, well, that didn't suit my interests here."

"I'll suit your interests. You want war, I can bring you war, mister."

Grant laughed. "How? You and some weeping widows?" He laughed harder.

"Grant, you son of a bitch, you don't pull in your horns I'll whack them off with a pruning saw. We'll see who laughs last. It won't be funny."

His round face grew red and he put his hands on his hips. "You ain't nothing but a drifting piece of shit. You better start drifting on or you'll be pushing up poppies."

"Have a real nice suit laid out for your services." Slocum turned the big horse and leading the other one headed out.

Still filled with raging anger, he short loped south. He hated that he had to leave Amantha there. Next he'd better drop by Myra's to see she was back and what was happening. Hungry and thirsty, he reached her place as the sun sank beyond the bloody red Dragoons.

"That you?" she called out, rushing to hug him.

"It ain't Geronimo." He dropped heavily to the ground.

Arms locked around him tight, her face was buried in his vest. "Damn, did you get her back all right?"

"She's home."

"Her father's good will lasted about two days. Then when you were gone they came back with a vengeance. One good thing— that boy you sent. He's staying at Sarah Kimes's house. He quit Grant over his double cross."

"Good. We have an ally."

"What's first? Food? Bath?" She looked up at him.

He kissed her hard on the mouth. *Who cared?*

12

Fresh from his hot bath and shave, he sat at her table in clean, waist overalls she'd laid out for him and watched her work preparing their food.

"She was very pretty."

"Amantha?"

"Grant's daughter." She twisted around and smiled at him.

"Very pretty. Hurt, but she'll recover."

Myra looked at the ceiling in disbelief. "I'd be hurt too. Rutted on, no doubt, by every buck in camp."

"It may slide by for her. She's hardy."

"Tough like her father?"

"No, she doesn't take after him. They don't get along well either."

"That's not hard to understood."

"They cut your fence again?"

"Twice and then drove cattle in my fields. I heard them and blasted cattle, raiders, and all with my shotgun. Had to fix more fence 'cause the cattle went out some other places that weren't cut, but they ain't been back since."

Slocum chuckled at her grit.

"You'd think they'd leave a woman alone," she said, still fuming.

"You simply are in their way."

"How?" She jerked around and frowned at him.

"He wants the entire valley."

"He can go to hell." She brought the dishes heaped with steaming green beans, brown beans, and fried ham to the table. Then she fetched the bread from the oven. Her light-browned soda biscuits that threatened to make his molars float away in the rush of saliva at the sight and smell of them.

"Riding all night to get back here, I imagine you're tired?" she said, sweeping her skirt and petticoats under her to sit down.

"Not too tired to eat."

"Good." She looked at him with a crooked smile. "Save an ounce or two of energy for your dessert."

He nodded and went to filling his plate. *Oh, boy*. There would not be much sleeping for him.

"I thought you needed to leave this country?" she asked, dishing food on her plate.

"Probably do. But I'm going to stay as long as I can to see this thing with Grant through."

They finished supper and she put the dishes on the dry sink. He leaned back in the chair, feeling heavy eyelidded when she whirled to face him. Her fingers deliberately untied the stings that held her skirt at the waist. In one swift move, she stepped out of it. The skirt safe on the chair, she began to undo the buttons at the waist securing her petticoats.

"I love how you watch me," she said, shedding them so the candle's orange light danced on her bare legs and hips.

"I always like it."

"Always," she repeated in a dry husky voice, stepping closer to him and taking the blouse off over her head.

Then she came and stood between his legs, cupping her breasts from the underside in his face. He pulled her closer and took the dollar-sized right nipple in his mouth. When he closed his lips on it, she gave a cry and clutched him to her, his tongue rousting her to more oh's and ah's.

Then she pulled his face up to kiss him. Her mouth felt a fire as she smothered him with her wet lips. He swept her up and carried her to the bed across the room. Her nipples felt like spearheads against him. Small fingers tore open his pants and forced them down to his knees. Then, greedy to possess him, her hands sought his half staff pole and cuddled his scrotum. A wave of newfound energy swept over him—gone was the weariness. Like a fountain of youth, it rose from his flank; she squirmed down on her back to receive him. Knees raised high, arms held up, she drew him down on top of her.

A steel hard erection parted her gates. His action drew a sharp cry from her lips as his hips pressed deeper into her. She raised her butt off the quilt to met his charge. Sweat soon greased their bellies. Coarse pubic hair rubbed hard between them as they both sought the depth of her cavern.

Her groans and hard breathing grew greater. Small hands gripped his forearms tighter and tighter as the walls swelled around his skintight invader with each plunge. She bucked harder and harder to meet his force. Then at the last minute, he went to the depths of her and spewed his relief in a great fountain that she succumbed to in a small pile beneath him.

She clung to him until he feared his weight would smother her, but she insisted and he savored the smooth skin and the feel of her luscious flesh against him. At last on the bed beside her, his eyes closed, he fell asleep.

Dawn filtered in the window and spread a yellow warmth on the floor. He pulled on his pants, looked at her sleeping in a fetal position. *Really overslept*—he went out on the porch and prepared to vent his bladder off the edge. Barefooted, he dared not venture any further than the edge for he wanted no goat heads or spines in his bare soles. Something was wrong. He turned with the chill of the morning wind raising goose bumps on his arms and saw the Apache squatted in his knee-high boots, army shirt, and breechcloth on the porch. His back against the clapboard siding.

"Caychem?" Slocum asked.

The buck nodded. "I was going to Mexico to warn you."

"Thanks. Everyone make it back?"

The scout nodded.

"Need money?"

The Apache's head shake made the freshly trimmed edges of his hair dance. "I come to help you."

"Help me?" Slocum frowned at him.

"Grant has a reward on you—dead."

Slocum shook his head in disgust. Unable to hold it any longer he undid his pants and began to piss a stream off the porch's edge with his back to the Apache. "When did he do that?"

"A few days ago."

"I was at his place yesterday. Him and I had war. So I guess it's still on me."

"Hmm," Caychem snorted out his nose. "Him not want to kill

you himself. Why he puts out reward? Easy, huh, get someone else kill you?"

"For him, I guess, yes."

"Why him mad? You find the girl and bring her back."

Slocum shook his head. "I ain't sure about the man or what he wants besides control of the entire valley."

"Who's here?" Myra asked from the doorway, wrapping a robe around her.

"Caychem came by to tell me that Grant has a reward out for me."

"Nothing shocks me about what that crazy man does." She turned and went inside after acknowledging the scout. "I'll fix you two some food. We about slept the day away."

"It was a good night's sleep," Slocum said after her and grinned at the Apache.

"What do you do next?" Caychem asked.

"I've been thinking if we can spook his hired guns off, he might leave the women in the valley alone."

"How we do that?"

"Put a rattlesnake or two in their bedrolls for starters."

The Apache grinned big and nodded he understood. "Give them plenty of sign."

"We'll start somewhere on spooking them." With a head toss, he started back inside.

"What are you two planning?" she asked, whipping up batter in large crock bowl.

"We're going to spook Grant's Texas rannies."

"They won't spook easy."

"We'll see. They ain't never been up against an Apache and a guy determined to put them on the road." Slocum showed the chair for Caychem to sit in, then took his own place. "What's to-day? I mean day of the week?"

"Friday, why?" she asked.

"Those guns of his will be in Tombstone or Wilcox on Saturday night."

She nodded. "I'd imagine Tombstone, but we need to get word to Jean Myers. If they go there they'd have to ride past her place, otherwise they'll be in Wilcox, but its mostly railroaders."

"Good, I'll ride over there and talk to her." He motioned to Caychem.

"You can scout around today. See where they are at and wha they're doing. Don't do anything, just get a line on his men. Ei ther of us need help, we'll set a single signal fire."

The Apache nodded.

"I'll go around and talk to the others and tell them not to shoo him." She indicated Caychem. "And to make smoke if they nee help."

"Good, tell them we need reports on his men's travels and what they're up to, too."

"You'll get that. We're having pancakes." She began to spoo the first batch on her griddle.

"Good enough." Slocum looked at the Apache and he nodde in agreement. No telling when Caychem ate last either.

After breakfast, Slocum borrowed one of her ponies and headed west for Jean Myers's place. Close to noon he rode int her yard. A dark-headed brunette in her twenties came out armed with a shotgun to stop him.

"Close enough, mister. Turn that hoss around and keep o riding."

He reined up the bay and gripped the saddle horn in both hands. "Myra sent me. Name's Slocum."

"Oh, I'm sorry. I thought you were one of them."

He dropped down and smiled at the three towheads who' managed to squeeze past her skirt to see who was there.

"We need a favor."

"What's that?"

"If Grant's gun hands ride by here for Tombstone on Saturday we need to know about it."

"They usually do."

"How many?"

"Three or four, up to ten. I guess it depends."

"Depends on what?"

"If they have any money or not left from their pay."

"Sounds reasonable enough."

"What are you going to do to them?"

"Make them want to leave the country."

"Wonderful idea if it works. Come in, I have some coo lemonade. You children stay out and play so I can talk to Mr Slocum."

Dismounted, he beat some of the dust off his sleeves and nodded to her.

"You can wash up if you need to." She indicated the pan on the stand and towel hanging by the door.

"I will."

"I wasn't expecting any company," she said, putting the scatter gun on a wall rack and then rearranging her dress. "That scurry bunch scattered my small flock of sheep last week."

"Get them back?"

"All but two ewes. The coyotes must've got them. Kids and I spent three days looking for them up there in the Dragoons." She bit on her lower lip.

Slocum dropped his gaze to the worn porch flooring and shook his head. "Real tough bunch, aren't they? Running off a woman's sheep."

Her gaze met his when he looked up. Her wide-open brown eyes told him enough. She'd use that shotgun on them if they ever came back.

When she took his hat, she indicated a chair at the table. "Bad enough to be a widow, I didn't deserve this bunch of bullies."

"No one does. I aim to try and stop them."

"Mister, you do—" She looked around to be certain none of the children were in the room. "I'd-I'd treat you to the finest time you've ever had."

"Not necessary."

Her face red with embarrassment, she spoke plainly, "I sure couldn't pay you, but I'd do my damnedest to see you were well taken care of."

"I savvy," he said and reached over to pat her forearm.

She sat on the edge of the chair and shook her head, about to cry. "Could—you hold me tight. For—just a minute."

"Sure." He rose and took her in his arms. Waves of trembles ran through her body as he clutched her slender form hard against his body.

"Sounds stupid, I know, but I miss just being held the most, I guess. Up there looking for those sheep with the three little ones—if someone had just hugged me like this—but you don't need to know about my troubles."

He rested his cheek on the top of her head.

Huddled in his embrace, she shivered more. "Oh, I'm so sorry."

"No, be calm. Your husband's gone?"

"Oh, yes—he divorced me and chose his youngest wife. Said she needed him worse."

He pulled her tight against his chest.

"The church is going to send us men, you know?"

"Myra said that."

"They'll no doubt be some English boys or old men that they've converted. What do you think?"

"I have no idea."

"Oh, Slocum don't quit holding me. Not yet."

He redid his hold on her. "An Apache is helping me. Whatever you do, don't shoot him. He wears a red headband. He'll show up and be squatted down and you won't hear a thing."

She tossed back her curly brown hair and looked up at him. "What's his name?"

"Caychem."

"I'll remember that. You need word if they ride by tomorrow?"

"Yes. Send up a smoke signal. I'll know what it is."

"Good, I was concerned how I'd let you know."

"Any time you need help, send up a smoke signal. One of us will come riding to your aid."

"Good."

"I'll make a stack ready with some green stuff to put on it. So all you need to do is set it on fire."

"Whew, thanks," she said, stood on her toes, and pecked his cheek.

He lifted her chin on the side of his hand and kissed her mouth. Her eyes flew open, then went shut in pleasure. When he finished, she fought to recover her breath.

"God's—come by any night—oh, damn."

He hugged her tighter and laughed. "We'll make this a better valley before we're done."

"I'd say so." She used her hand to sweep the hair back from her face. "Whew."

He picked up the glass of lemonade and took a deep draught of the sweet liquid. The coolness spread down his throat, cutting the trail dust and filling his mouth with saliva. He nodded in approval. Jean Myers would be a strong ally on the west side of the valley.

After arranging the fire stack, he left her place and rode back to Myra's. Midday, she was irrigating her alfalfa when he rode up. From under the brim of a wide straw hat, she grinned at him. Busy setting a small canvas dam to divert the next water set, she layered the edge of the cloth in the ditch bottom with damp dirt. Climbing out, she leaned on the long-handled shovel.

"Have any luck?"

"Jean's going to light a fire when they ride past her place on Saturday."

"What will you do then?" She started to open the ditch bank for the water to go in the field when she moved the set. He dismounted and took the shovel from her.

"I aim to make them so scared when they're in Tombstone, they'll lit a shuck and won't even ride back to Grant's."

"How?"

"Even tough men can be scared. Believe me."

When he finished the opening, she led the horse down the bank to show him where the other one needed to be cut in. That hole completed, they took down the set holding the water and allowed the liquid to flow in the new section and then spread out into the lush alfalfa full of noisy meadowlarks and killdeer. The birds were busy feasting on the bugs that climbed up to escape drowning.

"That will run all right until after lunch. Hungry?" she asked, sweeping the hair back from her face and holding it up to the south wind.

"I try to never miss a meal."

On the way to the house, he told her about Jean's sheep episode and she shook her head. "I sure hope that your plan works."

"It will. Any sign of Caychem?"

"No, he left for the mountains, I guess. Rode east."

Slocum looked over toward the hulking Chiricuhuas that touched the azure sky. No telling about the Apache—but he was no doubt learning all about Grant's operations.

"I need to ride down and see Easter Farley after lunch and tell her," Myra said.

"I can watch the water. I've irrigated before."

"I could tell that."

She threw her arm around his waist and bumped her hip against his leg. "Sure wish you were a stayer."

"Aw, we'd never get anything done."

She laughed and shook the straw hat on her head in the mirth. "Who'd care?"

"Not me."

"Only bad thing, I'll be so spoiled by the time you leave, I won't know what to do with myself."

"Sorry, this deal has no guarantees."

"I know. Kinda crazy, you find his daughter and he wants to kill you."

"Grant isn't always sane. Like what do a handful of women with small holdings mean to him anyway?"

"I don't know. But we've going to get company."

He could see the cloud of dust in the south, and emerging was a buckboard and a team. Too far away to tell.

"I think it's Sarah Kimes and that guy you sent. That quit Grant—Bill Gene?"

"Roy Gene?"

"Maybe."

Roy Gene reined the team up in the yard and blinked at Slocum. "Never thought I'd see you again."

Slocum nodded to the tall blond on the seat beside him and tipped his hat to her. "Good day, ma'am." Then he turned back to the younger man. "I'm fine. Grant's daughter is back too."

He would have sworn that the young man blushed with a look aside at his woman busy talking to Myra. The two were soon off to the house chattering at each other like magpies.

Roy Gene stepped down. "Been plenty happening around here since you left. I quit Grant. He never aimed to leave these poor women alone in the first place—he only agreed so you'd go look for her—his daughter, I mean."

"I found that out yesterday. You had any trouble?"

"Slick, Harve, and a greaser named Toro came by and warned me my life wasn't worth much if I didn't ride out."

"How many hired guns has Grant got?"

"Maybe a dozen tough ones. He had two dozen on the payroll at one time."

Roy Gene hitched the team to the rack and Slocum tied his horse up. Then he led the younger man to the straight-back chairs on the porch.

"What can we do?" Roy Gene asked, shaking his head. "He's got an army."

"One by one we need to discourage them. His gun hands and cowboys."

"How?"

Slocum looked around. "If you woke up and your privates were painted red and a note pinned on your chest says, 'Next time we'll cut them off,' what would you do?"

"I'd ride a horse in the ground getting the hell out of here."

"That's where we'll start."

"But how?"

"I'll find a way. Keep it a secret."

"I sure will. You need any help?"

"I've got an Apache scout helping, but I may later."

Roy Gene leaned on his knees. "Sure is a mess here. Sarah and I have considered leaving."

"That's what he wants."

"But she has two small children. Josie's watching them today while we went for supplies. Came by to see what Myra needed."

"If I was you I'd stay awhile longer. We might get lucky."

"Some of that bunch is double tough."

"We're going to play our game regardless."

"Good luck, but I can't see how one or two leaving out will help."

"How about a mass exodus?"

"I'd do what I could to help you do it."

Slocum figured, staring across the valley at the foothills, that Roy Gene would be limited help in his overall plan. All he would be good for was keeping the tall willowy blond company. Obviously he was enjoying the comforts of her shapely body too. The poor boy was simple enoughpussy whipped.

After lunch, the couple left and Myra rode over to warn her other neighbor Easter Farley about the consortium of one Apache and Slocum. He kept the sweet-smelling alfalfa company with the meadowlarks and shy pokes all around him.

Midafternoon, the Apache returned, came down to the field, and squatted on the bank.

"Cowboys at the cabin in Chiricuhuas on Turkey Creek." Caychem held up his hand to show five fingers. "Them just cowboys."

"Guess they'd get scared as hell over a real Apache raid on their camp?"

"Maybe shit in pants." Caychem laughed aloud.

"It'll be for a later plan. Saturday night, I want to scare some gunsels in Tombstone."

The Apache nodded. "You make gawdamn good farmer." He indicated the water set.

They both laughed.

13

Tombstone on Saturday night bustled with payday-rich miners, cattle rustlers, sleazy gamblers, and the riffraff that congregate in all sin cities of the west that Slocum could recall. Object number one was to provide all the sin-filled pleasures to fleece the workers of their money so they didn't leave their jobs in the mines and go home. That meant all kinds of debauchery was available, from the pony who screwed the girl on the stage of the Birdcage to the other doves in their cages above the noisy floor who for a fee accepted the same intrusion in their cunts from their unbathed customers. Independent whores working the streets to the more expensive ones upstairs in tented beds would have lines of eager horny men waiting for their sloppy turns at plundering womanhood's treasures.

With a sombrero on Caychem's head and the clothing of a peon to disguise him, he and Slocum left their horses in a dry wash north of town and climbed the hill after sundown.

Slocum told him to stay on the dim-lighted porch of Taylor's Mercantile and pushed inside. Miners were spending money under the coal oil lights on new clothing and footwear. A young clerk soon came over and asked if he could help.

"I need a quart of red paint and a brush," he told the young man.

"I'll get it right now."

"Good."

He paid the young man and went out to join the Apache. "Got it. You seen any of the crew?"

"They went in that saloon. One has a black leather vest. Got—you call cuffs."

"You know his name?"

89

Caychem shook his head.

"Hide our paint and this brush. I'll go over there. I've never met any of them. Maybe I can learn a thing a or two."

The Apache took the two items. "Me hide plenty good."

"Great. I'll be out of there in a little while. Keep an eye out for the Earps. They run the town. I know Virgil. He's okay. We don't need to tangle with them."

With a nod, Caychem was gone to hide the supplies until they needed them, and Slocum started across the street, dodging rigs and staggering men.

In the White Horse Saloon, Slocum spotted the black-vested Texan standing at the bar with three others that looked a little less dressed up than their partner.

He walked up as if looking for a place to slide in, met the Texan's hard gaze, and nodded. "You must be from Fort Worth?"

"By gawd, I've been there."

"Good to see someone from God's country," Slocum said.

"Get in here, pard, you're from Texas, we've got lots to talk about."

Slocum nodded and the big man introduced his crew.

"That's Earl, that's Tubby, that's Slick, and he's Stowker. I'm Ryhmer."

"Harley Holden," Slocum said. "Took several herds up the trail."

"You ever know John Blocker?" Ryhmer asked.

"Met him. He sure sent lots of cattle north."

"Biggest stockman in the Lone Star State. Most of us worked for John for years."

"Damn sight better man than the damnyankee we work for now," the chubby one called Tubby said and raised his glass of whiskey to it.

Ryhmer poured some in a glass and handed it to Slocum. "Here's to Texas and the fucking Confederacy."

"Amen!" went up in a chorus.

After another round, Slocum got ready to leave. "I've got me a little pussy up the street to see about."

"A little one?" Earl, the skinny one said and staggered a step or two until he was into Slocum's face holding his hand up in a fist. "That tight?"

"Gawdamn near."

"What's her name?"

"Annie."

"Gawdamn, all I ever find have got pussies big as horse collars."

"You need a bigger dick is all." Stowker gave the gun hand a shove.

"My pleasure, gents," Slocum said.

"You ever need work, come by Grant's ranch. He can always use a Texan knows how to use a gun. You know what I mean?"

Slocum nodded to the taller man and started to pay for his drink.

"Naw, the drinks are on Grant tonight. Some bounty man brought his daughter back from Mexico this week. You probably read where some renegade Apaches had kidnapped her. Anyhow he wants this guy killed now. Guess he raped his fancy little girl several times when he was bringing her back."

"Wonder how tight hers is?" Earl asked, showing off his drunkenness.

"I'd have screwed her," Tubby said, then tossed down another half-full glass.

They'd all be drunk in a few hours. Slocum still needed some notepaper and pins. Amantha never told her father a thing about their relationship on the trail. More of Grant's lies. The stupid man needed a .44 slug in his forehead—he might get one, too, before this was all over.

In the stationery store down the street, Slocum found some notepaper and then went to the mercantile for some safety pins. With a stub of pencil, he used a saddle seat at the hitch rail for his desk where the light from the open-door saloon shone out on the ponies.

This time it's paint—next time we cut them off. Get out of this country.

Earl was the first to stagger out the doors. Slocum and his scout followed him up Tough Nut Street until he collapsed to his knees. They swept in, one on each arm, and carried him the half block of boardwalk. By then he was passed completely out. Slocum put him over his shoulder and they dodged around a pile of tailings into the dry wash. He dumped him unceremoniously into the sand and gave a nod to the Apache in the bright pearly starlight.

Caychem pulled off his boots and soon had his belt undone.

Both men pulled off his pants as Earl on his back moaned in absent pleasure. "I sure hope you're tight, darling."

They quickly unbuttoned the bottom half of his underwear, jerked them away, and exposed his stark white legs and lower torso. On his knees in the sand, Slocum opened the lid on the paint can and generously painted the man's privates, belly, and the inside of his legs.

"Gawdamn—that feels—good, girl," Earl slurred in his drunken speech and then went limp.

The Apache pinned the note on his vest. Slocum closed the paint can lid. Their job completed, they headed up the hill, leaving the drunk passed out on his back in the dry wash.

Next, Tubby came out of the White Horse, stumbled, caught a porch post, and then looked around with bleary eyes. He was totally unprepared for the sweet thing that slipped under his arm and coaxed him away. She reached over, gave his privates a big squeeze, and laughed out loud.

"Jesus, what a dick you've got, honey."

"Big one—" he managed.

She half-carried him around the corner and up the alley. Slocum and Caychem took him from her after paying Sweet Rose two bucks. They laid him out in the dark alley, undid his pants, and exposed his privates. The Apache struck a match and Slocum skipped the brush this time, pouring the paint on the gunfighter's dick and balls. The second match went out and they both nodded satisfied in the shadowy light. On his knees, beside the passed out Tubby, Slocum pinned on the warning in the dark void of stinking refuge and yowling alley cats.

"That leaves Slick, Stowker, and Ryhmer," Slocum said when he straightened.

Caychem nodded. "Three more to give red balls to, huh?"

"Yes, if we can find them."

When Slocum glanced over the batwing doors into the White Horse's smoky room, he saw neither of the three in the crowd at the bar, their high crown hats an obvious signature of the Texans. *Damn where were they at?* Maybe the stables. They probably had bunks there. He found the street girl Sweet Rose.

"You seen three Texans?" Slocum asked her.

She squinted in the light filtering from the store window. "One went to Madam Ferdeuax's. The one in the fancy vest."

"That's up the street right?"

She held out her palm for pay.

Slocum put a silver dollar in it. "The other two cowboys?"

"I think one went to find a bed. I hit him up for a little and he said he was too drunk to get a hard-on."

He paid her the second silver cartwheel. "Which livery?"

"Pascals, I think. He went that way."

Slocum nodded.

"You or that Mexican with you want some pussy?"

He shook his head.

"What the hell you—"

His finger cut off her mouth; he leaned over and whispered in her ear, "We're castrating them, and if you don't shut your mouth up that Apache with me will cut your throat from ear to ear."

Her hand grasped her windpipe protectively and she paled in the night's shadowy light to a snowy white. "Jesus, I won't tell a soul."

"Good."

Then he led the Apache away. He didn't trust her not telling a thing. But by then it wouldn't matter. He wanted one more victim; then they could ride for Myra's place.

In the bunkhouse, full of sawmill snoring, they found Slick passed out in a lower bunk. Unceremoniously they dosed his privates good with the last of the paint and eased out, found their horses, and made the ride back to Myra's ranch.

The sun coming up behind the Chiricuhuas, she met them at the door.

"How was Tombstone, boys?"

"We painted parts of the town red," Slocum said, ready to wash his paint-stained hands at the washbasin she had set out for them on the porch.

With a quizzical frown at him, she laughed and went back inside. "You two are just in time for breakfast."

"Plenty good deal," Caychem said with a nod of approval at her announcement as he dried his hands.

"Plenty good," Slocum agreed. He wondered as he looked across the valley to the north, how many of them rode back from Tombstone with Ryhmer. That would be a good question to know the answer to. He rubbed his thumb on the red stain on the side of his index finger—be a good one to know, too.

"You find Grant's gunmen in Tombstone?" she asked, setting a platter of fried eggs on the table beside the browned bacon-stacked one.

"Yes, we did." He shared a nod with the scout.

"And?" She looked at the two of them, holding a platter of biscuits in the air.

"They probably have heads the size of a big horse today."

"What does that mean?"

"Well—" He paused as if pained to tell her. "Several of them have a new disease."

She scowled at them both. "What's that?"

"Called red belly."

"I never heard of that. How does it act?"

"Well—if you insist. It's the first sign your manhood is about to leave you if you remain in this country."

"I still don't understand?"

Slocum quit buttering a biscuit, sat back, and began to laugh. "They woke up this morning and everything below their belt was painted red and a note said, 'Next time we'll cut it off.'"

"Oh no. What did they do?"

"I hope they ran back to Texas as quick as they could."

Caychem had his head down, busy smothering his giggling.

"All right you two. Guess the war has begun?"

"No, it started when they drove cattle into your hay field. When they ran off Jean Myers's sheep herd. We have just begun to fight."

She nodded her head thoughtfully. "Guess no one got killed then?"

"We're doing all we can to avoid that."

"Good. While you two sleep today, I'll take some things over to Jean's and see how many rode back past her place today."

"Five rode down there."

"Is there enough food for the two of you?" she asked.

Both looked up and smiled in approval, then they went back to eating.

"Figured you'd be starved whenever you got back."

After a long nap, Slocum took a bath under her sun shower, an overhead tub she filled from a ladder and then let the solar heat warm it. He refilled it after his own usage and shaved after doing that. The day lengthened; with no sign of her return he began to wonder about her when she came trotting over the hill on her bay horse.

"Well," she said with a wide grin as she dismounted. "Jean only saw the one called Ryhmer return so far today."

He threw his arms around her and hugged her tight. "One small victory."

14

Turkey Creek Park was a remote place deep in the Chiricuhuas which rustlers had used years before to change brands on ill-gotten stock—horses and cattle. Most of those individuals had either ridden on or swung from a tree limb. The Grant Ranch hands, using the GFT brand, had been working cattle for the man. Lots of loose stock up in the canyons had gone unclaimed for years. The threat of an Apache outbreak and them sweeping down through that area was one reason. The absence of Brochious Bill made it safer to roam the mountains too. The onetime bandit leader, whom the Earps claimed to have shot while in pursuit of stage robbers, had simply disappeared from the region. Brochious's alleged reputation for murdering folks for their possessions kept the well-informed out of the mountains too.

Caychem reported that Grant's crew had set up housekeeping in Bill's old cabin and they kept a herd of cow ponies to ride. The horses were turned out of Bill's pens with a boy to wrangle them each day as they grazed, and he brought them back at night. Big steers were held in the pens and fed hay until they had enough to drive up to the main ranch. Cows and calves were driven in each day. The babies were cut, branded, and ear marked, then them and their mommas were turned out.

A smooth enough cow deal, Slocum decided, from the scout's description. Though he soon saw that many of the calves that bore new GFT brands, however, did not match their mother's scorched marks. Many were stray cattle that had hidden in the canyons for years, no doubt driven in there originally by rustlers. Several big bulls without marks were also cut and marked accordingly. The team worked smooth enough with a cook that stayed at camp and the young horse wrangler; five ranch hands did the hard riding, brush popping and working the stock as well.

None of the outfit carried the tough edge of Ryhmer and his bunch—still if they were going to bring Grant to terms Slocum needed to interrupt this operation.

"Can you make us some war paint?" Slocum asked, watching a rider disappear into the junipers and bring a horn-swinging half longhorn–durham cow and her big bull calf out on the flats.

"What color?"

"Red, black, and yellow?"

"Sure, what we do with it?"

"Scare the pants off that boy down there chousing that pair." Slocum was bellied down beside the scout on the ridge watching the gathering enterprise.

"Take me a day." Caychem stood and then disappeared.

Slocum scowled after him. Hell, he didn't have to run off just then, though watching them work cattle was getting old. He rose up and headed for his own horse. Be after sundown before he was back at Myra's.

"Where's Caychem?" she asked when he returned.

"Went off to make war paint."

"Huh?" she asked, looking all around outside the front door.

"We decided we needed war paint to scare them cowboys off. He ran off to make some."

"Oh."

"Hell, he just agreed to do it, got up, and rode away when I mentioned it." Slocum dried his hands. "You can't tell about what an Apache's thinking."

"Good, I have you by myself then." She hugged him tight.

"Wait. I hear cattle bawling."

She stopped and listened. "I hear them too. There must be several."

"Where's that scatter gun of yours?"

She reached behind the door and handed it to him. "What're you going to do?"

"Meet them head-on if they're going to try something. Turn out the lights. Keep the pistol of yours handy. You have any shells for this thing?"

Without a question, she ran inside and came back, stuffing his vest pockets with brass cartridges. "Be careful."

"I will. You stay down. I'll whistle when I return."

He left the porch as she doused the lights. In the starlight, he tried to see in the direction the cattle sounds came from. But the darkness absorbed any sighting as he ran downhill on his heels, jumped the ditch, and started across the field of half knee-high alfalfa plants. When he reached the north fence, he knew there were lots of cattle thundering down the valley and plenty of men driving them. He climbed over the four-strand barbwire knowing it would be no barrier to the onrushing herd.

To his left was a high point that he figured would be avoided by the stampede. The climb was tough, but he reached the top in time to see the wide front of charging cattle like a dark mat coming down the valley. Riders on both sides were shooting their guns in the air to hurry them onward. He drew the shotgun to his shoulder and began firing at any form. A rider went down. Another's mount, struck by the shot, left bucking into the night. They returned some pistol fire, but by then he was on his belly sending buckshot into the night at any red flashes of pistol shots.

The herd never stopped. The stretched barbwire screamed and then popped under the charge of the wide front. He knew, laying belly down on the rocks and sharp thorns, that their still thundering hooves were shredding and trampling her hay crop to nothing.

Damn you, Grant! Slocum was sprawled on the ground, his face in the alkali-tasting dust. If only he'd acted faster. Grant had rounded up a whole herd of old, toothless longhorn steers—not worth a dollar for their hides even—and stampeded them through her place. Shredding the whole crop. *Damn, you want war, you are going to get it.*

He staggered back to the house. When he came up the hill, she ran to meet him. In his arms, her tears soon soaked through his vest and they held each other, neither talking.

Daybreak, he hitched up her team and began the arduous task of shooting the crippled steers laying about the hay field with broken hips and legs, then dragging them out of the trampled alfalfa into the desert beyond her fences for the huge flock of buzzards circling over the farm. She soon joined him and drove the horses after he tied the chain on the dead steers' hind legs. While she was gone, he shot another crippled animal in the forehead between the eyes with his .44. Many acted mad, but the pistol quickly silenced any fight left in them.

By midday, Caychem joined them. He rode up on a new spotted pony and jumped down beside Slocum, who was waiting for her return with the team. "Who did this?"

"Who else?"

"I never seen so many buzzards." Caychem shook his head at all the birds boldly stalking about like soldiers among the dead cattle looking for an eye to pluck out.

"They'll have plenty to choose from."

"Why him do this?" Caychem made a pained face looking around at the carnage.

"To ruin her hay crop."

"I have the war paint."

"Good, maybe we get this field picked up, we'll have a war dance."

"Plenty good idea."

She pulled up the horses, swept the straw hat away, and wiped her forehead on her other sleeve. "Real mess, isn't it?"

"Bad thing," the Apache said.

"Real bad," she said and reined the team around and back to where Slocum could hitch the double tree to the next carcass.

"Me work them," Caychem volunteered, indicating the team.

She looked at Slocum for his approval. He nodded, then he started for the next animal. She caught the painted pony.

"I'll fix us some food. We need to eat," she said.

Pausing to reload his pistol, Slocum agreed. "That'll be fine."

She wet her lips and ran on.

A dozen head left to shoot. Then they'd need to drive the rest of the cattle off the place. What a mess. He punched in the fresh cartridges and started for an old mossy-horned critter obviously down in the hips for he sat up like a dog and bawled in pain. A lead slug soon stopped his misery.

They quit for lunch when she hollered the food was ready. Besides, the team needed a breather. They left them hitched to the rack in front of the yard and washed up on the porch. Myra came out to look over the havoc and shook her head.

"Losing that cutting of hay will hurt all right. But it's such a waste. All those old steers and barren cows and all."

Slocum paused, glanced back at the ones left, and agreed with a deep inhale. "He'll get his."

"What's the matter with him?"

"He's got some idea he's going to be king and control all of this valley, I guess."

"Come on, the food'll be cold. You two better eat."

They finished the job and repaired the fence breaks by sundown. All the old steers left standing were driven off and the night bugs sizzled when Slocum collapsed on the front porch. Stretched out on his side on the floor, he considered the soreness in his body and the tiredness in his pounding head. He watched her rock in the rocker with vengeance.

"There will be better days," he said.

"Damn, I hope so. Today wasn't one for sure. I'd never made it you two hadn't been here."

"Could have been worse."

"Only way was if my ex came by wanting to crawl in my bed."

"He do that often?"

"He tries. Surprised he ain't dropped in lately."

"Where's he at?"

"Up at Safford, north of here. It's a long drive."

"I'd sure come a long ways."

"Yes, but he knows now I'm not parting my legs for him anymore."

"You sound angry."

"I am. He took me for his wife before he took that little scamp he stayed with. But she always needed help. Guess that's what I get for being so efficient."

"Brigham Young will find you one."

"Brigham Young can go to hell too. If he thinks he's picking me a man, he's crazy."

"Lets go to bed."

She stood up and nodded sharply. "Let's. I want you to hold me tight."

"I can do that." He stood up stiffly and put his arm on her shoulder. *Be another day in the morning.*

After the steer episode, Slocum decided to ride around and check on the others before he started his plan to drive the cowboys off. He headed for Jean Myers, sending Caychem to check on Sarah and Roy Gene. Myra was to go by and see about Easter Farley. They were to be back at Myra's by noon.

Slocum short loped the bay horse all the way over and drew up to study the frame house from the ridge line. Nothing looked out of place. Wash on the line, the sheep were in the pasture. The steady wind was working her windmill.

He dismounted at the picket fence gate and opened it. *Where were the kids?* Too late, he saw the rifle barrel in the side window pointed at him.

"Make one wrong move and you're dead. Get 'em up."

His heart sank. He knew it was a trap. Slow like, he raised his hands, and the cocksure face of Ryhmer showed itself in the open doorway. His shoulder to the facing, he chewed on a toothpick.

"Get up here."

When he passed the man, Ryhmer jerked his Colt out of the holster. "I think you know Mrs. Myers."

Tied in the chair, her eyes rimmed in red from crying, she looked sad and crestfallen.

"I'm—sorry," she managed.

"Think nothing of it," Slocum said, as another ranny he didn't know came over and tied his hands behind his back.

"I wondered who you were in Tombstone," Ryhmer said, clapping his black leather gloves together like a man about to do something. "You've damn sure costed me some good men. But that's all right. There's more where they come from."

The ranny forced Slocum to sit on a high-back chair. Then he tied his feet and hands to the chair.

"This lady needs a lesson. See, she don't learn good. Today she's going to learn what happens to women that don't do as they're told."

Slocum sized the two men with Ryhmer. One that was burly built, blond-headed had tied him up. The other he recognized from Tombstone. Kinda Ryhmer's right hand—Stowker. They'd all do to watch.

"Get her on the bed," Ryhmer said, pulling off his gloves. He turned back and smiled. "We saved this for you to see."

"You harm her and you're dead."

"Tough talk for a guy that may never live to make that threat good." Ryhmer set his black hat on the table, then began to undress. He neatly put his gun belt beside Slocum's six-gun, then the leather vest and his hat.

Meanwhile, Jean was powerless, hauled over by the strong

arms of the pair, and they thoroughly thrust her down on the bed. Her cries and protests speared Slocum's heart as they stripped away her skirt and slips. Soon her bare white legs flashed as she tried to kick them, but her efforts were useless.

"Hold still, you damn bitch!" The one Stowker called Larson swore and a resounding clap of him slapping her silenced her to whimpers.

"You ain't seen nothing yet, you little Mormon whore," Stowker said.

"Hold her down boys," Ryhmer said, undressed and stroking his dick with one hand, crossing the room. "I get this poker in that wild cat, she'll know what a real man feels like. Oh, yeah, enjoy yourself watching me, Slocum."

With all his might, Slocum strained at the binds. He only saw black as the Texan climbed on the bed, parted her flailing legs while they held her down and he moved between them.

"No, no!" Then there was silence as Ryhmer began to stuff her with his dick.

Through rage-filled eyes, Slocum watched the man forcefully gather her legs up and hunch deeper into her. His grunts grew louder and louder until he finally came and fell off.

Stowker already had his pants to his knees and climbed on the bed quick as a cat. He was inside her as she moaned and groaned under his efforts. Cheering him on, other two laughed and made vile comments. Their attention was centered on the bare-assed cowboy still wearing his boots and spurs, busy raping the slender woman's body.

On the table was Ryhmer's silver-studded holster set and Slocum's own handgun—less than five steps away. But even if the rope around his wrists would give enough, instead of cutting into his wrists like knives, how could he, tied to the chair, ever get to the firearms in time. It was a chance he had to take. One more sum bitch left to rape her, whenever the horny Stowker finished with his part.

"You bitch, you'll learn to get out of this valley when we get through with you."

The rope gave a little behind Slocum's back. He could feel the warm blood trickling down his fingers. No time to stop; listening to the ring of Stowker's spurs as he drove harder and harder into her. The rope gave some more.

"Where's her lard at?" Larson demanded, breaking the attention centered on her rape.

"Over there," Ryhmer said. "I'd guess. What for?"

"Hell, that damn Stowler's wearing out her out. I'm going to use her ass."

"Good idea," Ryhmer said and glanced back at Slocum with a grin. "Bet you'd not thought of that."

All Slocum could do was grimace and glare back at the man. Precious seconds went by, and Larson returned to the scene with the green pail before Slocum could start working more on his ties. The ropes were giving some or the slickness of his own blood was making them less tight. *Still not enough.*

Stowker about fell down getting off of her and the bed with his pants wrapped around his legs. He shook his head and looked as dazed as Ryhmer had. Neither man looked back at Slocum. Larson had removed his boots and pants, when they flopped her over on her stomach. He took a fist full of lard and applied it to his rigid dick, then climbed on the bed.

"Don't! Don't!" Jean cried, but forced facedown on the bed by the other two, she had little effect on what happened next to her.

With one giant effort, Slocum ripped his hands free and the pain shot through his arms and shoulder.

Jean's scream of terror and pain shattered the room when Larson tried to shove his hard-on into her ass. He grunted and then drove his hatchet ass hard to her. His success came as the shrill, desperate cry escaped her mouth.

Slocum saw they were centered on this brutal act and his feet touched the floor. One, two steps carrying the chair he was bound to, and then his freed hand clasped the familiar Colt. Trigger cocked, he looked into the shocked eyes of Stowker.

"You son of a bitch—"

Last words from the hired gun. The lead projectile hit him square in the chest and flung him against the dresser. In the bitter black gun smoke, Slocum aimed at the fleeing Ryhmer, but knew the next two shots only drew holes in the wooden door facing. By then the bitter blinding fog filled the entire room

Cussing like a sailor, Larson scrambled across the floor on his hands and knees to reach the window and dove outside before Slocum could get off the next shot. Then, still seated, Slocum could hear the sounds of their horses rushing away. They were gone.

He dropped the gun on the floor and shook his head in defeat.
Then woodenly he undid the rest of the ropes. Residual gun
smoke burned his eyes and he went to where Jean lay sobbing
across the bed.

"They're gone."

"Bastards—bastards—"

"Yeah. They'll pay for this."

She rolled over with a look of pain on her face and reached for
her backside in discomfort. "Oh, he hurt me."

He sat on the bed and hugged her bare shoulder. "I couldn't
get loose any faster."

"Oh, you're bleeding." She frowned, looking at his cut wrist
on the arm around her neck.

"I'll be fine. Where are the children?"

"Oh, my God. They locked them in the chicken house. They
must be in despair by now." She began to scramble around for her
clothing.

"You dress. I'll go get them."

On her knees, atop the bed, she clutched her petticoat slips to
her pear-shaped breasts and shook her head in defeat. "Thanks.
I'll try to be together when you get back."

"Their names?"

"Horace, the oldest, Mathiew, and Symirnah is the youngest."

"Good." Slocum started for the backdoor.

"Tell them momma is all right."

"I will."

He crossed the yard; there was no sign of the other two. They
were long gone up the valley somewhere. The south wind making
the windmill sing swept his face and bare head. Ewes bleated to
their lambs. He combed through his rumpled hair and reached the
shed.

With his boot, he kicked away the stick holding the door shut
and drew it back.

"Horace?"

Three wide wet sets of eyes peered up at him.

"It's all right now. Those men are gone."

"Did they hurt mother?" the eldest of the three asked.

"No, she'll be fine."

"We heard her scream."

A cold chill ran from his jawbone to his eye. He tried to form the words, but they came slower than he wanted. "She'll be okay."

"Good," Horace said and took the kids' hands in his. "This place stinks. We may need a bath—how come are your hands bloody?"

"I cut them."

Horace nodded. "Mother said knives would cut you."

"Yes," Slocum said, herding his wards for the house. "I should be more careful."

15

Slocum tried to recall the exact layout of Grant's headquarters. He'd worried about the whole thing the entire ride back to Myra's. How could they best invade his main headquarters? Maybe Caychem knew how.

There was a strange horse hitched at the rack when they approached. He and the Apache shared frowns. Then they shrugged the notion away and rode in. Dismounted, Slocum looked up. Standing on the porch, his striped pants tucked in high-top black boots with a silver deputy star badge pinned on his vest, stood Billy Pritchard. It had been five years since Slocum had last seen him.

"You two's under arrest for shooting and killing Matt Stowker."

"How do you know we killed him?" Slocum asked.

"Cause two guys told the judge in Tombstone you shot him down in cold blood."

"Last time I seen Stowker he was drinking whiskey over in Paradise. Right Caychem?"

"Him drink plenty whiskey."

"Sheriff said to bring you both in."

"Guess Behan and Grant are close friends. The sheriff being the tax collector and all."

"I never mentioned Grant."

"Well, that's who Stowker worked for."

"Slocum, that ain't getting you out of going in. You handing over your gun or we having it out?"

"Considering I don't want any of Jean's young'uns shot, reckon I'll go along."

"How about you, Injun?"

106

Caychem shrugged and shook his head. "You got good food there?"

Myra elbowed by the deputy. "Sorry, Slocum, I had no way to warn you."

He shook his head to mildly dismiss her concern. "If we'd killed him, then they got to find the body to prove we did it."

"We'll find the body," Pritchard said, taking their guns.

"I'm starved," Slocum said, ignoring the lawman.

"Food's about ready. Get out of my way, badge toter. They gave you their word." She backed him through the doorway and then hurried off to her range.

Slocum spotted Jean keeping her children in a huddle in the far corner.

"Horace, you doing all right?" Slocum called out.

"Me fine," the boy said back.

"Good, how's your mom?"

"I'm all right." Jean quickly nodded and stood. "They said they sure appreciated you letting them out of that smelly old chicken house."

"I bet they were glad." He strode across the room to where they were at.

"We never told Pritchard a thing," Jean said, from behind her hand.

Slocum nodded. "They're speculating."

"Supper's ready," Myra announced.

"Where in the hell did that damn Injun go?" Pritchard demanded, whirling around. His eyes wide open with a scowl on his face he ran to the front doorway.

The two women suppressed grins and ducked their heads.

"You can't ever tell about a damn Apache," Slocum said. "Here one minute, gone the next. Of course, he might be out in the yard or waiting behind the yard fence. You can go look for him if you want. We're going to eat."

"Slocum, you aren't even funny." Pritchard's right hand on his gun butt, he glared across the room at Slocum.

"Didn't aim to be." He walked over, took out a straight-back chair, and seated himself. "You better eat too. 'Cause you can't track that buck on an empty stomach and he's long gone besides."

"You distracted me." Pritchard pointed an accusing finger at him.

Ignoring the deputy, he began to fill his plate. "That wasn't hard. Hell, I was talking to a woman who's had her flock of sheep run off by this bunch. Who's had her house broken up by these so-called hired guns that you're defending, and you blame me for letting one short buck get away." He passed the green beans. "Pritchard, you might ought to turn in that badge."

"Shut up!" The deputy stepped astraddle a chair and took his place.

"Just being informative."

"Why didn't she file a report?" Pritchard glanced over at Jean, still holding her three little ones aside.

"What good would that do? Her word against them liars."

"Behan—" Pritchard used his fork to point at him. "The sheriff don't want a range war up here."

"Range war ain't the word for it. There's several widows up and down this valley and one fat rancher up there at Wilcox Station. He wants to control it all."

Pritchard shook his head, busy fixing his plate. "We never heard a word about it until—"

"Until Ryhmer and who else came in?"

"Some hand named Larson," Pritchard said, between bites he shoveled in his mouth.

Slocum shot a glance at Myra. She shook her head in disapproval. This jail business could be serious. His absence would leave the women exposed to any trickery that Grant or Ryhmer had on their minds. No telling where Caychem ran off to. He looked at the mashed potatoes and gravy on his plate. *They damn sure won't have any of that in the Cochise County Jail either.*

"If neither you nor Behan ever heard about the trouble up here, how come he's worried about a range war starting?" Slocum sat back and looked hard across the table at the deputy for his answer.

"The killing of Stowker brought it up."

"That's their side of the story. You have two liars' word on it. Nobody else's."

"You said that before. They know where the body is they say."

"Good, make them bring it in then. Maybe they shot Stowker and want to pin it on me."

Ready to shovel in another bite, Pritchard paused and looked around like a trapped man. "That's the judge and prosecutor's business, not mine."

The next morning with Slocum's hands in shackles, they rode for Tombstone. Before they left, he assured Myra they had no case.

"Don't matter. I'll get you a lawyer," she promised.

They reached Tombstone after lunch and dismounted before the new courthouse. Pritchard guided his prisoner inside and had him registered in the jail.

"Can't say it was good to see you again," Pritchard said as the turnkey was about to take Slocum back to the cell block.

"Guess the feeling's mutual, Bill. Don't take any wooden nickels."

Pritchard never answered him, and the jailer led Slocum into the cell block.

A couple hours later, Johnny Behan, dressed in his tailored suit and diamond stickpin in his silk tie, came to the cell bars.

"Pritchard tells me he knows you."

Slocum sat up on the bunk and combed his too long hair back with his fingers. "We knew each other in our Kansas trail driving days."

"Never been there. You could plead guilty to manslaughter and get two years in prison."

"That the best deal you got?"

"The only one I'll make. I don't know what's going on up there, but we ain't having no damn range war."

Slocum walked over to the bars, grasping them in his hands. Behan was shorter than he recalled. "Maybe raping innocent women, running off their flocks of sheep, and stampeding cattle through a woman's hay crop is good fun. Your friend Grant's not a nice guy."

"Who was raped?"

"A damn nice woman, Ryhmer, Stowker, and Larson raped her. They also ran off her small flock of sheep. They locked her three little kids in a chicken coop, too."

"That's why Stowker's dead?"

Slocum looked hard at lawman. "I don't know he's dead. Last time I saw him he was drinking whiskey in the bar up at Paradise. Maybe he went back to Texas. Folks do those sort of things."

"We'll see."

"They need to produce a body to try me for murder."

Behan never answered; he started down the cell block for the door. He stopped and turned back. "Them's strong accusations."

"Ride up there and ask them. They'll tell you all about it."

Behan nodded. "I may do that." Then he left the jail with a clang of the iron door.

Slocum went back to catching up on his sleep. No telling about the sheriff, whose side he would land on, between his tax collecting efforts and siding with the Clantons—maybe he wasn't that close to Grant, either. Slocum stared at the tin ceiling, *Just no telling.*

A lawyer named Sam Elliot came to see him. A balding, red-faced man who mopped his sweaty face with his kerchief and acted pressed for time sat outside the bars on a straight-back chair the jailer had proved him.

"I've been to Judge Isaac's office and demanded a writ of habeas corpus. His secretary said they're planning on holding hearings Friday."

"What's that mean?"

"They'll bring in witnesses and evidence and try to show cause for your indictment."

"What about bail?"

Elliot shook his head. The disheveled-looking man dropped his gaze. "Behan says you're too big a risk. You'd skip for Mexico."

"He might be right. They do need a body for murder charges, right?"

"Exactly."

"Heresay evidence won't convict me."

"Not of murder." Elliot gave him a weary look and rose to his feet. "The charges are still serious. Mrs. Downing wants to be sure they don't railroad you."

"I appreciate her."

Elliot looked around. "I had no idea the problem those women have been having. I've wired Salt Lake." He glanced at the other prisoners in cells nearby and, being sure there was no one in earshot, lowered his voice. "I asked Brigham Young to send some Avenging Angels."

"Will he send some?" Slocum had heard about the gun hands hired by the Mormon Church leader to protect individuals of the church under attack. Looked like he might learn all about them, if he ever got out of jail.

"I think so."

"Mrs. Downing, Myra, tell you the whole story?"

"Most of it I guess." Elliot rose to leave. "I am sending over a barber and someone to fit you in a suit for the hearing."

"Sounds more like a funeral parlor."

"No, I want you to make as good an appearance as you can. Maybe we can get the whole thing squelched at the hearing."

"Thanks."

"Need anything?" Elliot was standing up with his white shirttail half out of his waistband and his suit coat in disarray.

Slocum shook his head. No sense asking this son of Moroni to bring him some cigars to smoke. They didn't believe in tobacco.

Friday crawled into view. The haircut and shave left him smelling like rose oil. The tailor found a good used suit for him to rent, a new white shirt and tie to wear. So he was ready for the hearing when the guard took him upstairs to the courtroom.

Elliot nodded in approval at his appearance, taking a seat beside him at the table. Slocum turned and gave a nod to Myra in the gallery, then he twisted around to sit with his hands clasped on top of the table.

Formalities were soon over and Judge Isaac called the prosecutor forward.

"Cause for this hearing?"

"Your honor, the prosecution intends to demonstrate to the court today, how this man, John Slocum, did with malice shoot and kill one Matt Stowker."

"I object your honor." Elliot popped out of his chair with his motion.

"Overruled. We have not heard a thing about this matter, Mr. Elliot. What can you possibly object to?"

"There is no corpus dilecti. To have a murder, you must first have a body."

"Mr. Cantor, is there a body?"

"Your honor, we are currently searching for that body."

"Counselor has a point. If you wish to charge Mr. Slocum with murder then we will need a medical examiner's report."

"I have three eye witnesses ready to swear they saw Slocum shoot the man."

"Your honor." Elliot was on his feet again. "That is not evidence of the crime."

"You have made your point, Mr. Elliot. Both counselors need to meet with me in my chambers."

Elliot nodded to Slocum and in a low voice said, "We have them on the run. Those Grant's men on the front row?"

Slocum glanced over and saw Ryhmer's black leather vest. Then he nodded.

Elliot made a sign that was good, then wrinkled his nose like they were out of place. Obviously he held lots of faith in dressing up to appear in court. Slocum gave a tug on the sides of his suit then sat back. If dressing up would win, they might.

After fifteen minutes, the three men returned.

The judge rapped his gavel. "It is the opinion of this court that the evidence available is insufficient at this time to proceed. Mr. Slocum, you are to remain in Cochise County until this case can be resolved. Matter of bond has been set at one hundred dollars. Are you prepared to provide that amount at this time?"

"We are, your honor," Elliot said.

"Very well, I shall dismiss today's hearing until such time as the prosecutor wishes to resume. Mr. Slocum, I suggest you remain in the county until this matter is resolved."

Slocum nodded and turned as Myra rushed in and hugged him. "You're free!"

"Well, sort of." He extended his hand behind her back to Elliot and shook it. "Thanks."

"No problem. I'll send word if anything changes."

Slocum agreed, but he was busy watching the three hired guns in conference with Cantor on the other side of the aisle. Ryhmer's cold, hard look was wasted on him—but he knew since this scheme to have him tried for murder had failed, they'd try something else.

"Let's go home," Myra said.

"After we eat a meal at Nellie Cashman's. After this jailhouse slop, I'm starved for some real food," he said.

"I guess we could call it a celebration."

"Yes," Slocum agreed and watched the three hard cases storm out the back of the courtroom.

16

Virgil Earp wore a thick mustache, black suit, and a small badge on his vest. His hard, coal-dark eyes squinted in the corners from the harsh Arizona sun's glare, even shaded under the flat brim hat.

"Heard they let you off?" he said, leaned against the porch post in front of Nellie's restaurant. Earp was staring across the street at an adobe house.

"Judge dismissed it temporarily for lack of a body." Slocum stopped behind the man.

"Can they find the body?"

"I doubt it."

Earp nodded, then recognizing that Myra was with him, quickly removed his hat. "Sorry. Thought he was alone, ma'am."

"No problem, Marshal." A smile crossed her face under the brim of felt hat she wore.

"Myra, this is Virgil."

"My pleasure." Virgil made a small bow. "Any friend of Slocum is sure to be welcome in Tombstone."

"Myra has a ranch in Sulfur Springs Valley. Raises alfalfa."

"Interesting. Wyatt needs some hay for his racehorses he has stabled."

"I'll have new cutting in a few weeks. A stampede trampled the last one."

"Sorry to hear about your losses." Virgil turned to Slocum. "Watch your back. Ryhmer used to work for Ike Clanton. He took the higher paying job being Grant's *segundo*."

"I didn't know that."

"Thought you should be warned."

"Can we buy you lunch?"

113

A small grin creased the corners of Earp's tight face. "After that jailhouse garbage I bet you're ready for a real meal. Take you up on it next time. Good day, ma'am." He touched the brim of his hat and walked away.

"You know him well?" she asked.

"Well enough. Virgil's one you can count on in that family."

She glanced back after the man and nodded. "I never knew anything about them, but the rumors."

"Plenty of them floating around. Lunch comes next." He showed her through the doors into the fragrant food smells of Nellie's place.

After a fine lunch, they left Tombstone in her buckboard. It felt good to be wearing his six-gun again. The team was fresh and held to a good trot off through town and northward.

Time the sun was ready to set behind the Dragoons, they were driving into her place.

"You seen any sign of that Apache since he ran off?" he asked her as he reined up at the yard gate.

"He's up there on the porch waiting for you." Myra hugged his arm and laughed as the ex scout rose and stretched.

"I'll be damned."

Caychem joined him when he was ready to unharness and put up the team.

"No one came back to Turkey Creek. Place still empty."

"Good. What are Grant's men doing?" Slocum asked jerking the harness off the near horse.

"Staying close by his place. Maybe one or two new ones up there."

"More gun hands?"

"He hired some Mexican cowboys, too."

"You know them?"

Caychem shook his head. "They won't go up on Turkey Creek. Too afraid of 'pache spirits up there."

"What good will they be to Grant?" He slung the harness on the corral and helped the Apache do the same with the other set.

Caychem laughed. "Maybe eat his beans."

"No, Grant's plan does not include these women staying here."

Caychem threw up his hands for no answer. "How was the food in jail?"

"Bad, let's go eat some of hers."

• • •

The next morning they rode to Jean's place. She and the children looked settled back in. Easter Farley's son Carl had ridden home to check on his mother and was due back the next day to stay and help her.

"He sure likes the saddle you gave him."

"No one recognized it as Stowker's?"

She grinned and shook her head. "No, but they dug enough holes around here to bury everyone in Tombstone."

"You should have made them fill them up," he said looking in disgust at piles of dirt.

"Carl says he can take a slip and refill them when he gets back."

"Seems like a nice young man."

"Very nice. Sure is a big help to me. I'm so glad Sister Farley let me have him to work over here."

Slocum had forgotten how LDS women called each other "sisters." He decided things were fine there, so they headed back for Myra's after he left some candy for the kids. Jean looked disappointed that he wouldn't stay longer, but he wanted to see how the others were doing—and look for signs of Grant's next attack.

When they reached Myra's, there was a strange horse tied at the yard fence. Slocum reined up on the the ridge line and felt for the butt of his Colt. He gave the Apache a head toss to circle in from the back.

With a nod, Caychem bolted his pony into the junipers and started to work his way around to the backside. Slocum gave his spurs to the bay and started down the sandy incline for the house place. Her wash was flapping in the breeze on the line. The windmill creaking away on the sucker rod, pumping water out the pipe into the tank. Things looked well in control, save that horse tied at the gate.

He dismounted heavily, using the bay for a shield, adjusting the position of the Colt, and looking around for any other sign.

"You made it back," Myra said with a smile from the doorway. "Come in. We have a friend of yours here."

He blinked his eyes. Amantha Grant stood in the doorway in a divided riding skirt, her face a soft tan and even her blistered nose healed and smooth-looking.

"How are you? I heard about the frame-up they tried," Amantha said, looking uncomfortable standing there until he held out his arms to hug her.

"Yes," she said very defiantly and clutched him tight.

"What else do they have in mind?" he asked, taking one of them under each arm and going in the house.

"They've sent for two Kansas deputies to come and arrest you."

"Lyle and Ferd Abbott?"

"Yes, that's why I came to warn you," Amantha said.

"Who in the hell told them about the Abbotts?"

Myra shook her head in disgust. "From what she told me, Pritchard told them about the warrant for you and her father paid him the reward for giving him the information about the bounty."

"Pritchard, huh? Those two are the reason I can't stay long in one place." Slocum shook his head and chewed on his lower lip. What must he do next?

There were two rapists—Larson and Ryhmer—still on the loose. He needed to settle with Grant over his raids made upon the women. No telling where those two Kansas deputies were at—could take them a week or two to get there. He needed to make some plans.

"I'm going to marry Charles Rambolt," Amantha announced. "I can't stand living another day in my father's house, and all he has on is mind is owning this whole valley. He is obsessed with the idea."

"You can stay here anytime. What're you going to do?" Myra asked Slocum.

"I'm not certain. But I can't stay here much longer with the Abbott Brothers coming."

"Mexico?" Myra asked.

"Closest place," Slocum said, then nodded toward the scout standing in the back doorway. "It's all right."

Amantha planned to spend the night at Myra's. Slocum wanted a last look at Grant's headquarters before he pulled out, so he had her draw him a detailed map. When she finished, he and Caychem took fresh horses and headed for Winslow Station and Grant's hacienda.

They reached the place after dark, moved in from the grass-mesquite flats to the back of the corral system. Easing their way through the pens of young Durham bulls getting acclimated to the climate before they were turned out, Slocum turned an ear to some woman's hysterical crying.

"Something is wrong here," he said to the Apache, and they climbed over the fence running up the starlit alley ways. Six-guns in hand, they reached some ramadas and listened.

"The *patron* is dead!" a woman's shrill voice announced as she ran by holding up her skirts.

"What?" Slocum asked Caychem.

"She says the *patron* is dead."

"She mean Grant?"

"I think so."

"Come on, we better go see for ourselves."

They hurried to the main house. The front door stood open and the lamps were lit in the great living room. Slocum paused in the vestibule and looked around. A wet-eyed Mrs. Daggett came running.

"Those bastards killed him," she said.

Slocum caught her arm. "What bastards?"

"Ryhmer and the other two. Come, I'll show you."

"Lead the way." He gave a head toss for his man to follow.

They rushed into a side room where several hatless vaqueros stood around the bed, looking very grave. She pushed some aside for him to see the bloody-chested, pale-faced Grant.

"They shot him."

"They take anything?"

"All the safe held I guess—" She led him by the arm to look at the open door of the large green safe and the bare insides, save for some loose papers.

"How long ago?"

"Three or four hours ago, we think."

"Ryhmer, Larson, and who was the third man?"

"Wallace," she said.

"I'm taking fresh horses and going after them. Someone must ride up the valley to the alfalfa fields and tell his daughter Amantha about his death. She is staying there tonight with Mrs. Downing."

"I'll send a rider right now." She turned and talked in Spanish to one of the vaqueros.

"Someone also must ride for the sheriff too. In Tombstone. Tell Behan who did this and that they are headed for Mexico. I think he is too late to stop them, but tell him anyhow."

"What else must we do?" the woman asked.

"Cover him and wait for the sheriff to come."

"Where will you go?"

"I have a score to settle with Ryhmer."

"I understand, and do that for all of us here, too." She turned and sent a boy after two good horses for them.

Saddles switched to the frisky new ponies, the two headed south, knowing that Ryhmer and his sidekicks was no doubt making a beeline for Sonora. They needed no tracks. The way the killers took was apparent. Ryhmer would never stop close to the border either—he'd be deep into Mexico before he ever reined up.

17

Fronteras would be Ryhmer's first stop south by Slocum's calculation. Things began to add up to that answer as the two rode south. A goat herder across the border told them he saw three gringos, one wore a fancy leather vest, ride by the day before headed south. He grinned big at the two ten centavos coins that Slocum paid him.

"They're still ahead of us," Caychem said when they left the man and his bleating wards.

Slocum nodded. "Means we're on their tracks, too."

"I figured those tracks were the ones I saw up there."

"You're a wonder, my friend. What makes an Apache so good at tracking?"

"From a little boy on that is what they teach you. Was that lizard running or walking across here."

"How do you know?"

"They twist their feet to run so the print is messed up more. Walking, it is a good print."

"Score one for you. Next time I track a lizard I'll know that." They both laughed.

Slocum's eyes were on the set of desert foothills to their right. If Ryhmer and company did like he expected they'd skirt the range, stick to the desert, and eventually go around them. They would also no doubt stop at Hienrich's place. Depending on his latest arrival of whores, they might or might not stay there a night. If they did, he and Caychem would catch up with them there.

"They're going around the hills, aren't they?" he asked the Apache, who was off his horse looking for sign on the ground in the greasewood flats.

At last, his scout nodded, grabbed a hunk of mane, and swung up on his horse. "They were trotting their horses too."

"Then we better do that too."

The sky dripped blood in the west when they came into view of the German's place. Deep red shone on the walls of the compound. Slocum felt for the Colt, undid the tie down on the hammer. A good chance they'd meet up with the threesome there. Their sweaty horses, bobbing their heads to snort and flinging sweat, began to walk the last quarter mile. Slocum glanced over his shoulder at the scene behind him—nothing out of place. As long as Ryhmer didn't have a sharpshooter posted somewhere on those walls ahead, they'd be all right.

The low slanting sun in the gunner's eyes might be an advantage for the two of them. His worked-up pony danced sideways, heading for the settlement.

"Guess he's ready for a bait of feed."

"I liked Myra's best. She always have plenty food."

"Me too, pard. What I really hate about a place like this is the beans always end up being gritty."

"Eat plenty sand, huh?"

"I've damn sure ate plenty of it." Slocum made a wry look at his associate. One thing he hated—bits of sand on the surface of his molars.

They rode through the gate, Slocum looking around and knowing that his partner was also on edge. Nothing out of place in the small square, they dismounted heavily at the well with the trough to water man and beast.

"Well, what brings you hombres to Hell?" The woman speaking to them came out the open doorway and stood with her hands on her amble hips as if to challenge them.

"A good piece of ass," Slocum said and with a grin, nodded in approval at his companion.

"Well, you came to the right place. Phillippe, put their horses up," she ordered.

A boy of ten rushed out and took their reins.

"Any other gringos staying here, boy?" Slocum asked under his breath.

"No, they left this morning." Slocum shared a questioning look at the Apache.

His diamond eyes searched around the empty square then he nodded. "Their tracks went out."

"All of them go?" Slocum asked, counting out the coins in his palm for the boy.

"*Si*, three hombres."

"One wear a leather vest?"

"Black one. He was the boss."

"Boss, huh?"

"Yeah, he hit one of the others in the mouth about something."

Slocum gave him the two ten centavos pieces. "You take good care of them horses."

"Oh, *si*," the boy said, thrilled at his payment. "I will brush them down and feed them myself."

"Sunup, I want you to have them here." Slocum pointed ot the ground between his boots.

"*Si*, senor."

"Come on, Caychem. We better see how good she is."

"You want food first?" she asked.

"We can start there. Tell me about the gringos that left here," he said as she gathered both of them by the arm and herded them in the cantina.

"They were cheap bastards."

"Oh, they paid you well?"

She looked up at him with an impatient smirk. "You know them, no? They wanted me to fuck for fifty cents."

"That's all they would pay?"

"For three of them, too?"

"My, there are no other girls here?" Slocum looked over the bar with the dusty mountain sheep head on the wall. A cracked mirror on the back bar and a thin-faced bartender who was polishing glasses.

"*Carrumba*! The others all ran and hide when they hear them talk about being so cheap."

"Find my amigo a pretty girl, and we'll all have some food and drinks."

"Juan, bring a bottle," she said to the bartender. "This hombre wants to party."

"I will go get this good-looking caballero a fine pullet," she said and sashayed off to find her.

Slocum nodded, took off his hat and hung it on the wall, wiped his sweaty forehead on his dust-floured sleeve, and motioned for Caychem to sit down.

"They're already in Fronteras. We rode all night we'd get there in the daylight. May as well spend the night here and ride there tomorrow and get there in the dark. Then they won't see us coming, huh?"

Caychem grinned. "Damn good idea."

"Hey, hombres, this is Nita," she said, pulling the dark-skinned younger girl behind her in the room.

"This is Caychem. I'm Slocum." He took the bottle the bartender brought over and set on their table and splashed liquor in the four glasses. "What's your name?"

"Mayletta." The buxom proprietor stood before the table, lifted the glass, and looked directly in his eyes. "I drink to your health and a great erection, grande hombre."

"Couldn't drink to anything better in my life." He and the others clunked glasses.

"Juan, have the old woman kill a goat. We are having a fiesta tonight. Get that boy in here too," she shouted after the barman. "He needs to play his guitar. I want to dance."

A very old woman brought them a huge bowl of crisp tortillas, loaves of steaming, fresh oven bread, and bowls of red salsa to eat. The liquor flowed. Soon the barefooted Phillippe sat on a large drum and played a Spanish guitar for Mayletta to dance to. She stomped around a sombrero, and clacked castanets in her fingers. Her dark eyes framed by long lashes never quit looking at Slocum—challenging him with her quick sharp movements, the amble breasts shaking under the thin, low-cut blouse.

Slocum dipped a hunk of torn-off bread in the salsa then moved his mouth under it. Fire and treasure, the sourdough's richness and the hot peppers' sharp flavor going out his nostrils like a fire-breathing dragon. This was Mexico at its best. Strong liquor, women that stomped their heels, the guitar music, and good food.

Juan soon brought out a fiddle and began to accompany the boy.

Slocum looked over at his scout with his arm around the Indian girl Nita. They were busy talking. No problem there. The music continued. Soon Mayletta had him up waltzing, holding her tight, so her breasts drove into his rock-hard belly as they swung around the room. Even on the gritty floor their steps went smoothly.

They paused for another drink. Then she told her two-piece orchestra to continue. Slocum looked up when a vaquero wearing a straw sombrero came in and removed his big hat.

"Ah, we are having a fiesta!" the new one shouted and looked pleased.

'Si, hombre!" Mayletta told him, leaning back in Slocum's arms so the edges of her brown dollar-size nipples were exposed over the top of the low-cut blouse.

"I will get my trumpet!" And he was gone out the door, to return in seconds with a beat-up tin instrument. Slocum doubted anything like music could come from such a battered horn. But he was wrong. The trumpeter was an expert and what blew from his mouth flowed in with the others' music like when two great rivers collided into one.

"Ah," she said, looking up at Slocum. "Now we have a real fiesta. I better tell her to kill two goats."

"How much are they?" Slocum asked.

"Oh, a peso for the fat ones."

"Tell her to kill four," Slocum said.

"Wonderful, amigo! You are a great lover." She crushed herself to him in a hard squeeze and then swung away to run over, stand on the brass rail, hang over the bar top, and shout over the music to someone in the back. "*Quatro* goats. You hear me?"

"*Si, si quatro.*"

"*Buena!*" Then she made prancing steps coming back, waving her arms seductivly over her head and sticking her ripe melons out front. "Oh, hombre, we are going to have fun tonight."

Juan lit more lamps and the old woman brought platters of goat, apologizing she had more on to cook. Two younger girls joined them. Both were new to the business, Mayletta said, but she was teaching them. Two more vaqueros came through the batwing doors and looked delighted to be in on such a fiesta.

Mayletta introduced them as Piquell and Eduardo. They took off their sombreros and bowed their heads to him. "*Gracias*, senor, for inviting us."

Slocum ordered more bottles of mescal and everyone nodded in approval, the musicians taking time out to eat from the platter of tasty barbecued chunks of *cabretto*. With greasy smiles, they tore off more hunks of fresh bread and stuffed their mouths with it between bites of the flavorful meat.

"What are you in Mexico for?" Mayletta asked, sitting in his lap.

Slocum looked away. "To get those three bastards who rode through here yesterday."

She nodded and then squirmed on top of his leg, so he could feel the lips of her vagina through the thin skirt material. "I hope you blow their brains out."

He acknowledged he had heard her.

With a chunk of fire-browned meat in her fingers, she carefully fed him a bite of it, taking small nibbles herself after him. "We don't get many men like you here. Ones ready to have a real fiesta."

"My notion about that"—Slocum took and other bite of the tender kid—"I may not have another one, so I better have them while I can."

"And in such great company." She waved her other arm at the crowd. "Good people."

"Real good." She leaned back and kissed him on the mouth. "Let's party!"

In a short while, Caychem and Nita disappeared. A vaquero took one of the other younger girls down the back hallway. The trumpet player was being jacked off by the third *puta* in a booth in the shadows at the edge of the ring of light over them.

"Come," she said to Slocum and pulled him to his feet. "Time for us to go find a bed, too."

She led him down the hallway and passed the curtained doorways. With her finger to her mouth, she tossed her head at the next curtain. Then she pulled it away so they could spy on the young couple on the bed.

The thin, naked form of a young vaquero had the *puta's* slender legs split wide and he was giving her hell. His grunts were real efforts and she cried underneath in pleasure's arms.

She wrinkled her nose, let the curtain fall back, and with toss of her head for him to follow her, led the way to the end of the hall. There she unlocked a real door—thick and made of oak. It creaked heavily on the hinges. Inside, she shut it and bolted it quickly after him, submerging them in darkness, save a small window's starlight coming in the upper wall.

Her fingers began to peel off his clothing. He toed off his boots and felt his pants slide down the sides of his legs. Her hot breath on his stomach, she knelt before him. Her small fingers hefted his half erection as if weighing it. Quickly, she began to lick the head with increased enthusiasm, her lips closing around the ring. He shot up on his stocking toes to try to escape her wanton hunger, but she only took more of his rising shaft, teasing the underside harder with her hot tongue.

When he became fully engorged, she was forced to back off and could only take the cap of it in her mouth. She cradled his testicles and her fingers gently squeezed them. Then she tore way and led him to the bed.

The bed's ropes complained when she guided him between her silky legs, scooting anxiously underneath him and pushing his hard shaft through the butterfly lips of her cunt. When he shoved the nose cone through her ring, she cried out and threw her head and arms back on the bed. "Jesus of Mary! What a grande hombre!"

His hips ached to charge her and they did. Their bellies became slick with sweat as they fought for pleasure's highest peak. The walls inside began to swell and soon the effort became harder and harder to penetrate her.

He felt the sharp pain of two hot needles in his butt and drove home. The explosion that ripped the head of his dick showered hot lava inside her. They both collapsed in a spent pile.

He slept for a while and awoke to discover she was gently pulling on his spent rod.

"Will he awaken?" she asked on her knees beside him in the dim light.

"Maybe." He fondled her melon-sized breasts and savored the attention.

"Maybe? I want him again."

"You have to be patient," he teased her, feeling the return of power.

"Ah, he is coming now," she said, sounding confident.

When his erection grew stiff enough, he scrambled out from beneath her and spread her legs apart with her on her hands and knees. He waded up closer to her butt and reached around to ease his hard-on inside of her fire box. Pushing and pulling, he worked it in until she began to murmur, then he reached under her and caught her clitoris between his thumb and forefinger. The hard button was larger than most and she cried out when he found it. Gently jacking on it, her erection grew larger. He increased his movement in and out until she dropped on her elbows crying out, "Oh, yes! Oh, yes!"

She stiffened and then she came in a flood of hot liquid that ran over and dripped off his dick and balls. Like he'd blown out the light, she crumbled on her face under him and fainted.

"No hombre," she mumbled laying on her side. "Even when I was little girl and peed in my pants because I wanted so bad for boys to fuck me. Never did one of them ever do what you did to me tonight."

"How old were you when that first happened?"

"Maybe ten."

"Ten?"

"Listen, my lover, when I was five this boy lived next door, he put his finger in me. That was all it took."

"All it took?"

"Oh, *si*. All it took. After that I wanted more."

"More?"

"He couldn't, but he had an older brother, twelve, who had a small weenie one."

"He did it to you?"

"Some. Then when I was eleven, there was boy fourteen. He could do it forever."

"You ever get caught?"

"Oh, my grandmama caught me all the time fucking some boy. She would whip me and the poor one I was doing it with with peach branches and then she'd lock me up. But I didn't care, when I got out I found another pecker."

"So what happened next?"

"She got tired of it and made me marry a man who she knew needed a wife."

"How old were you then?"

"Twelve, thirteen. He was thirty."

"Were you his wife long?"

"Not for long. He would get drunk and bring his compadres back to the casa and they would all screw me and give him the *dinero*."

"So?"

"So why should I make him the money? I threw him out and kept the pesos they paid me."

"How did you get here?"

"I was going to the border and found this place. The German needed someone to run it. He hired me."

"Where's he at?"

"Mexico City on business. He won't be back for a month."

"I need a drink," Slocum said, getting up and pulling on his pants. "To the lady, I salute."

She scrambled out of bed in the darkness and wrapped a duster around herself. "I know the good stuff."

"Sounds all right," he said and put his arm on her shoulder as she unbolted the door. They trudged up the hallway, past the rooms of grunting couples, and found the barroom empty. She ducked under the hinged position, found a bottle, and brought it back.

"Here's to your health, hombre." She poured the two glasses half full.

"Here's to yours."

They drank up and Slocum looked around. *Not a bad fiesta.* When he was riding across the desert in the damn heat with a bad hangover the next day, looking for Ryhmer, he could always tell himself it had been a fun time with Mayletta.

18

Slocum's head hurt worse than he had ever imagined it would. The sun boiled down on him and his companion who had thrown up three times since leaving the place until the problem forced the Apache to stagger along beside his horse and stop repeatedly for the dry heaves.

"Helluva damn party," Slocum said and slapped the saddle horn.

"Oh, my head hurts," Caychem moaned and about fell face-down in the tan caliche between the greasewood brush.

"It'll have to feel better when it gets better." Slocum shook his head, hungover, his pecker sore from the friction burns and abuse. His lower back ached from all the pounding he'd given her—damn him and that Apache made a helluva team.

By nightfall and after a siesta under a ramada some generous Latino lady rented them for three ten centavos pieces as well as feeding them some of her spicy meat burritos wrapped in flour tortillas, Sonora style, Slocum felt better.

"You know someone in Fronteras?" Caychem asked.

"*Si,* Magdelania Morales."

"I hope she don't want to party tonight."

"I can't say, but she will know if those three are here."

"Whew, I could sleep some more."

"I agree, but we will see what she knows first."

With the scout to his left, they rode up the dark, narrow street, their shod horses' shoes ringing occasionally on the rock base. Slocum indicated a large wooden gate. He pushed the horse in close and pulled the bell rope that rang a small brass one.

"Who is there?" a voice asked.

"A friend of the senora's. Slocum."

128

"Slo-cum?"

"Yeah, she knows me."

"I will check."

They sat their horses and waited a few minutes. Slocum turned his ear and listened. Talking inside at a hundred miles an hour in Spanish, her familiar voice scolded the guard.

"You dumb donkey, of course, I know Slocum. He is one of my dearest and best friends. Why have you left him standing in the street? The poor man has ridden miles to see me."

The gate swung open and the buxom form of Senora Magdelania Morales stood feet apart, blocking their entrance in her fancy ruffled dress.

"Where in the hell have you been, hombre?" she demanded.

Slocum slipped from the saddle and took her in his arms to hug and kiss her. "Me and Caychem"—he pushed his hat up with his thumb, his nose full of her expensive French perfume—"Have been riding day and night to get here."

"Liars!" Then her olive face broke into a pleased smile. "Take care of their horses. Anita!" she shouted to a girl on the balcony. "Draw two baths. They smell worse than dead horses."

A stable boy took their reins, and Caychem looked around at the courtyard like a man lost. Slocum assured him they were safe there. The buck nodded in approval.

She took Slocum guardedly by the arm and led him toward the lighted, open French doors. A thousand bougainvillea flowers gave a scent in the air that masked the city's raw odors.

"Come along. You can see this place later," she said over her shoulder to Caychem.

"I'm after three gringos that rode into town today I think. They'll be in the barrio. Tough and dangerous."

"What are their names?"

"Ryhmer, Larson, and Wallace."

She stopped and turned. "Rafael, go and get the boy Ramon. I have a mission for him to do for me."

"Si, senora." The man ran off across the cobblestones for the back part.

"Ramon can check the barrio out and get your answer. What did these men do?"

"Raped a young mother, locked her little children in a chicken coop, and murdered a man."

"Real *bastardos*. Come, the baths will be ready. Some clean clothes then we can eat, no?"

"We can eat," Slocum agreed, and Caychem did the same.

She showed them to the tiled bathing room and both men quickly undressed. She gathered up their clothing in a bundle and paid little attention to them stepping in the tub. When she handed the laundry out, she told another girl to come and help her get these *caballeros* clean.

Armed with soap and a long-handled brush, Magdelania started scrubbing on Slocum's back, and the other girl she called Teeyah began to work on the Apache's. They were swift and efficient. The cold rinse water poured over the men's heads soon shriveled up any partial erection and Magdelania laughed about it.

Red-faced, Teeyah rushed away. A houseboy delivered starched clothing to fit them. Of course, the senora always kept sizes big enough for Slocum; the shorter Apache was the average size of most Mexican men—no problem for her to fit him.

When they were dressed, she led them down the hallway to a great table. "I told that boy to learn all he could about them."

"Wonderful," Slocum said and hugged her shoulder.

"You know whenever you're in Fronteras where to stay?" she said to Caychem.

"*Si,*" he said quickly.

"Any amigo of Slocum is welcome here," she said over her shoulder to the Apache.

"*Gracias,* senora."

The large table was set, and the boy waiting on them poured red wine in silver goblets. She directed Slocum to sit in the head chair, the uncomfortable-looking Apache on his right and and her on the left corner.

The food she served them would have fed an army. The fire-seared beef served on screwers must have came from a large, milk-fed calf. Plenty of grilled onions, sweet peppers, hot ones, browned tomato slices, and lamb chops. Flour tortillas thin as paper and hot from the griddle to wrap and ladle things. A rich chicken soup thick as oatmeal. Slocum never realized how hungry he was, despite the noon meal with the lady on the road.

"Ramon is back," the waiter announced.

The boy, dressed in white cotton clothing, came and stood at attention before her.

"So, what did you learn?" she asked sharply.

"The three men are in Loco's Cantina. They are drinking lots and—"

"And what?"

"They were busy with the *putas*."

"There. You are a good worker. You may go now." She gave him a flat-handed slap on the butt and laughed after him.

"Thanks," Slocum said to the boy before he retreated to the kitchen.

"Let them get good and drunk. In a few hours, you can go down there and drag them in. We need more wine." She used a silver spoon to ring on her water glass for the waiter. "Bring more wine for my guests."

Slocum agreed.

"What will you do with them?" she asked.

"If we can take them alive, we'll take them back to stand trial."

"They will be desperate men, no?"

"Yes, I imagine so. For killing a big rancher and stealing all his money, I imagine they'll get the death sentence."

"You have an hour," she said and took him by the hand. "What about your friend?"

"I think he only wants to sleep that hour." Slocum looked over at his man, who quickly nodded in approval.

"I have girls."

"No. He wants to nap."

She shrugged "whatever," threw back the ruffles, and led Slocum down the hallway.

Their tryst in the goose-down bed was soon over. Naked, she laid on her back cupping her full brown breasts and shaking her head. "I always think—I don't care if that damn Slocum ever comes back. But when you do—" She sighed. "I am always grateful. You be careful capturing these hombres."

"I will, lovely lady."

After midnight, Slocum and Caychem set out with their guide Ramon, who earlier had reported where the threesome was head-quartered. Through the dark streets, past many drunks and even some drunken *putas* who rushed out and rubbed their palms over the boy's crotch.

"I can fuck you good," the streetwalker would say. Quickly, he would reject them with a rough shove aside as if insulted that they would even dare interrupt his mission.

From the shadows across the street, Slocum surveyed the place. No doubt the three spent horses at the rack belonged to the outlaws.

"Loosen the cinches on their horses first," he hissed at the Apache. "We may need them to carry them back to Arizona or I'd cut them. Ramon, you can go home now. We can handle this."

"The girls' rooms are in the back," the boy said. "You can go in the alley and go in the rear door and you will be in the kitchen. The hallway to their rooms leads to the cantina."

"Thanks, we can find it." Slocum nodded to Caychem and they crossed the street. Undoing the cinches, they searched around, the noisy music and girls screaming came out the lighted front entrance shielded by the batwing doors. In minutes, the two with their six-guns drawn were slipping in the sour-smelling kitchen with a few flickering candles to light the area where the doves must eat at a long table. After Magelania's fine food, the smells of this place reminded Slocum of a slop parlor. They walked softly on the greasy tile, and when he reached the end of hallway, he looked through the smoky yellow light from the saloon portion and small lights along the route.

Which room were they in? He hoped to find Ryhmer first. That would be like getting an ace on the first card dealt—not likely.

"Stay here," he told Caychem. "And cover me."

At the first curtain door, he could hear lots of grunts and effort. He stepped inside the cloth barrier, let his eyes adjust to the starlight, and stepped beside the bed. A white-skinned man was working hard to plunge his way with a dick through a teenage *puta* under him.

"Don't make a sound," he said, realizing he didn't know the man. "You Wallace?"

"Yeah, who the hell are you—"

Slocum bashed him over the head with his gun and he collapsed on top of the girl, who got out half a scream before Slocum's hand cut it off.

"Hush, I won't hurt you," he said close to her ear.

Her bug eyes wide open, she nodded that she would. He holstered his gun and helped her out from underneath him. The curtain parted and to his relief, the Apache slipped in.

"It's all right," Slocum whispered at the girl when she sucked in her breath at his appearance. "Which room is the guy in the black vest in?"

She shook her head, arms clutching her small breasts and standing back as the Apache ripped up her sheet and quickly bound the moaning outlaw.

"Wallace—where the hell are you?" someone shouted in the hallway. It was Ryhmer.

Slocum drew his six-gun, waving the *puta* into the corner where she crouched and whimpered in fear.

"Wallace, we're getting the hell out of here," Ryhmer shouted again.

The sounds of soles on the gritty tile floor made Slocum think those two were leaving. He stuck his head and six-gun out. Shots rang out. The percussion put out the lights. *Putas* screamed in fear, and Slocum knew they were getting away.

Maybe the loose cinches would stop them, but they must have drawn them up because by the time he fought his way through the milling throng in the saloon, they were riding away in the night. *Damn*. He had one, but the other two were gone.

They took the grumbling Wallace back to Magdelania's place for the night, locked him in a secure room, and found beds to sleep in. Pursuit of the others would have to wait.

In the morning, Slocum considered his options. Send the prisoner back to Arizona with Caychem—no, he better go along himself. To Mexicans, it might look strange for an Apache to be holding a gringo prisoner.

After breakfast, he interrogated Wallace.

"Where's you boss headed?"

"How the hell should I know?" The Texan had a slant to his gray eyes that told Slocum how hard cased he could be.

"Maybe a little Apache torture would refresh your memory."

"I told you, I don't know. He mentioned some place called Roses."

Slocum looked at Magdelania, who stood arms folded by the doorway.

"That could be anywhere."

Slocum agreed. "We're taking you back for murder and robbery."

"You ain't got no gawdamn authority in Mexico, lawman."

"Oh, I'm not the law. I am taking you back. One wrong move out of you and that Apache will deliver your head to the Cochise County sheriff."

"You're the bastard he spoke about—Slocum from some where up there?"

"That's me."

"Well, I know one thing, Ryhmer going to kill you sooner or later."

"Or I'll kill him."

The outlaw shrugged. "I'd bet on Ryhmer."

"We'll see." Slocum rose from the bench and nodded to her. "I need to send a wire to Sheriff Behan to meet us at San Bernadino in three days and we'll deliver his killer."

"Write it down. I will have Ramon send the telegram."

"Good. We'll need to buy a horse for him to ride. His has been ridden to death and not cared for."

"I will have the livery bring one in the hour."

"I can pay you—"

She looked displeased at him. "Keep your money. You don't look rich yet to me."

"Oh, I am with beautiful women like you to care for me."

"Apache, has he been in the sun a lot lately?" she asked.

Caychem, about to smile, bobbed his head. "*Si*, much sun."

They left Fronteras at sundown that evening to cross the desert in the cooler hours. A quick stop over at the German's place the next night with Mayletta. At dawn they headed for the border and San Bernadino. Wallace proved to be a big grumbler about everything and finally shut up only when Slocum promised to tie him belly down over the thin horse bought for him to ride back.

Behan came across the border and met them. In his fine suit with some trail dust on the sleeves and shoulders, he looked over the prisoner with his hands bound sitting on the floor. They talked inside the jacal that Slocum rented for the day from a small widow woman. She left it to them, clutching her two pesos he paid her, and went to stay with her sister. Through some missing teeth, she assured him that her kin would be glad to see her. Then chuckling over her windfall, graciously left the place to them.

"Well, Wallace, where are your buddies?" Behan asked.

"Go fuck a rock."

"He don't know," Slocum said. "Ryhmer mentioned Roses, but we couldn't find out anymore than that."

"Maybe you'll find him," Behan said and started to hand over a hundred-dollar reward.

"Give it to him," Slocum indicated the scout. "I've got more fish to fry than Ryhmer. He'll show up again. You'll get him."

Caychem frowned at Slocum over the money that Behan counted out to him.

"End of our road, hombre. You can use it." Slocum waved at him to take it.

"All of it?"

"Sure."

The payment complete, Behan turned and looked at Slocum. "By the way, those Kansas deputies were sure disappointed you were gone when they got down here."

Slocum nodded. "I bet they were."

"You two walk him down there to the border and shove him across. I'll be on my way."

"Gag him," Slocum said to the Apache.

"You guys can't do this!" His protests were soon muffled by Caychem's gag around his mouth. Slocum jerked Wallace up by the collar and headed for the door, half dragging him. "The sooner you get this mouthy sum bitch in your custody the better I'll like it."

19

His pockets flush with reward money, Caychem decided to go up on Cibeque Creek and see about an Apache woman who lived up there on the reservation. He rode across the border the next day, leading Wallace's horse Slocum had given him and waved good-by.

After the scout left, Slocum saddled up his horse, strapped on the bedroll, and considered a short ride up into the Sulfur Valley to see how Myra and the other widows were getting along. If those Kansas deputies were gone, maybe he could get in a quick visit and then fade back south of the border.

He needed to ride over the Mule Shoes and slip into the Sulfur Springs Valley at night. Not many of the sparse residents in those mountains asked many questions if you weren't rustling their stock. In fact, several big-name law breakers passed through them coming and going on the outlaw railroad out of Montana, Wyoming, Utah, and then Arizona on their way to Mexico. Same path lots of renegade bucks used to go from the Sierra Madres to San Carlos to see relatives and family.

By midday, Slocum was well into the canyon country and making his way up a trail. Above him, he spotted a rider on horseback, sitting his mount as if waiting for him to climb the trail before he went down it. The man wore cowboy gear, so Slocum wasn't too concerned still—he wondered about why he didn't start down. There was room anywhere to pass.

When he drew up closer, something familiar about the man made Slocum wonder.

"You're sure a sight for sore eyes, hoss." The familiar grin and twinkling eyes of Tom Horn made Slocum grin back.

"What brings a Pinkerton man to this end of hell?" Slocum took off his hat and wiped his sweaty forehead on his sleeve.

"A bank robber named Billy Twig." Tom looked over the desert country behind Slocum's back and shook his head in disappointment.

"How far you tracked him?"

"Six weeks. Lost him twice."

"I never saw him between here and Fronteras. I just came from there, and he wasn't on the road."

"Damn." Horn slapped his saddle horn with his palm. "He doubled back on me."

"Maybe he went to Silver City."

"You might be right. Maybe I better check over there if he ain't in Mexico. I know a rancher over on the east side of the Chiricuhuas where I can spend the night. Where're you headed?"

"Oh, up the trail here a ways."

Horn accepted that as an answer. The two rode north together a short distance, talking about the days of the Apaches war before they shook hands and parted. Horn rode off to the east with a wave. "Keep your head down."

"I will."

There was a light in the kitchen when Slocum crested the rise. He swung wide and came up behind the corral and pens. His horse hitched in back of some junipers, he moved closer in the starlight.

Then, at a man's voice, he stopped and listened. "I dare say Myra, this Arizona is different that I—"

A smile in the corner of his mouth, he covered it so he did not laugh out loud. Brigham had sent her a husband no doubt. Carefully, he retreated to the shed and dug up Grant's reward, stowed it in the saddlebags, and checked the cinch. When he swung up, he wondered if Jean Myers had a new man yet.

He rode west toward the hunkered down shadowy shape of the Dragoons. In a few hours, he saw the light on in her house. *Good—someone was still up.* He dismounted and started up the trail to her place through the grass and sagebrush.

From the porch, he could hear the creak of the rocker. A dog barked and he stopped.

"Who's out there?" Jean asked, sounding alerted.

"Friend," he said and by then the stock dog was all around him.

"Slocum? That you?"

"Yes, don't shoot."

"I wasn't expecting you. Did you find those—killers?"

"One. The others got away again."

She met him at the foot of the stairs and buried her face in his vest.

"I came by Myra's."

"Did you meet that Englishman?"

"No, but I heard him."

"She hasn't married him yet. But I told mine I was perfectly fine here alone and he could go stay in Tombstone or wherever. I don't care if it makes the whole damn church mad."

She looked up at him hard in the pearly light of night. He kissed her. She returned the same.

"I'm afraid we'll wake the children inside." She looked around furiously, searching for a aput. "I know. We can go use Carl's bed in the barn. He's at his mother helping her this week."

"You sure?"

She drove a feinted fist in his gut. "I was sure the first day you held me."

In the hay and barley-smelling small tack room they shed their clothing in the dark. Then she slipped into his arms, and he held her slender form tight to his chest. The small, hard nipples felt like nails into his skin. In seconds, they were on the bed, making the frame creak as he pounded his rigid tool inside of her. She moaned and tossed her head in wild abandonment. Then she began fighting for her breath, clutching him until her fingernails dug in his forearms like claws, and cried out, "Yes, yes" until he came inside her.

"I won't ever have some prissy Englishman in my bed," she said, squirming underneath him to savor their attachment. "I want a real man."

Braced above her, Slocum smiled at her. She threw her slender legs up both sides of him. "I could handle some more."

He stayed the night at Jean's. At sunup, he gave her half of the money Grant paid him for the reward, and her eyes about popped out.

"You can't—can't. Why, this is a fortune."

"That's enough money to get you and the kids by until you find that right man, isn't it?"

"God's, yes, but what will you do?"

"I don't need much. You think Myra would want to marry that guy if she had the other half?"

"I doubt it."

Slocum shoved the rest of the sack of money across the table. "Give it to her. No holds barred. She can do what she wants."

"I know damn good and well, she'll throw him out. All she's scared of is that bank payment since she missed the hay cutting."

"She don't have to." He shook his head. "That's all."

Jean climbed on his lap, put her arms around his neck. "You ever ride through here and don't stop to see me I'll horsewhip you."

"Sounds serious. How's Amantha doing with the ranch?"

"She's not getting married. I think she was only going to do that to escape her father. Him gone—" She looked hard into his eyes then impulsive-like kissed him.

"What about the kids?"

She wrinkled her nose. "I don't care who knows about us, Slocum."

He laughed.

20

For the next few weeks, Slocum drifted around northern Mexico. Then he dropped in and spent a week of rest and relaxation at Magdelania's in Fronteras. There was no word of the other killers since they rode out—like the desert had swallowed them.

Then a friend of hers called on him one day. Gilberto Reyes, a stout-looking short man in a white cotton suit with a gold-topped walking cane.

"My darling Magdelania tells me you are a big hombre and now I see you, I say she is right."

They sat in woven willow chairs on the upstairs balcony overlooking the courtyard, sipping good wine. Birds sang in the palm trees and small purple Sonoran doves danced in the fountain below. A breeze swept them better than the paddle fans throughout her house, run by belts and a steam engine in the backyard.

"You have mines?"

"Si, many, but to sell silver and gold is always a risky business. You can take high-grade ore across and not pay any tax at the border. Ingots are taxed 20 percent or more. And the best prices are in dollars, of course."

"Of course."

"But to get such rich ore to the smelters is dangerous business."

"You want to send ore to a smelter across the border?"

"American one, yes."

"So you want to ship ore up there? Where?"

"Silver City, New Mexico?"

"Why do you tell me this?"

140

"There are many bad men on the border. They have robbed many of my trains."

"So you need some guards to get them there?"

"*Si,* senor. I need someone who can get it there. I have lost several shipments. So I need to get some up there or go broke."

"When?"

"When can you go?" Reyes raised his silver goblet.

"Today."

Reyes's eyes flew open "So soon?"

"No one knows about it right now, but you and me. Start making a fuss and you will be swarmed with bandits, right?"

"Oh, yes. You will take shipment up there for me?"

"It'll be expensive."

"If you can deliver it, I can afford the costs. What will they be?"

"A half dozen men at, say, at a hundred American dollars apiece. Some dynamite, food supplies, you can supply the mule packers or I can get them. I want big stout mules, not burros."

"You get the packers. I don't know about the big mules—"

"I can find them. We'll have to be quick as a cat or else we'll get caught."

"I see that."

Slocum folded his arms over his chest, sat back, and looked hard at the man.

"What if someone at your mine tells the bandits?"

Reyes leaned forward and frowned at him. "Where do you get such ideas?"

"Hey, this is my neck, not yours."

"It is my money."

"Good, then you be sure of your people. Where's the ore?"

"At my mine in the Madres."

"I'll round up a crew. How many mules?"

"Bring what you can—this ore is almost pure gold and very heavy. We could never get it all on one train, anyway."

"I'll get what I can."

"*Gracias, mi* amigo. You have made my day. When will we speak again?"

"Week to ten days. I may need some mules and supplies paid for at the border."

"I will give you some bank drafts."

"Fine. The sooner the better. Be less talk about it."

• • •

A week later, Slocum sat on the front porch of John Slaughter's house and ate popcorn with Buffie. John was gone to to Socorro, New Mexico, to see about some cattle contracts he needed filled. The afternoon breeze swept the shady, east-side porch and the chattering of children playing and splashing in the irrigation ditch carried to them.

"How many more men and mules do you expect?" she asked, gathering a handful from the bowl.

"I can go with the number I have now. I'm waiting for my Apache scout Caychem to get here."

"Where's he?"

"Oh, he's been courting some Apache woman up on Cibeque Creek, I guess."

A warm smile spread over Buffie's handsome face, and before she tossed the kernels in her mouth she smiled at him. "He may be so struck, he doesn't come along."

Slocum shrugged. "Then he gets left."

Jones, Posey, and four more skinners they'd brought with the mules were at the ranch using the buildings and pens over in Mexico that John let Slocum use to assemble his train. Five of his Apache scouts were there too.

If Caychem didn't show up, they'd leave in the morning without him. They would go directly to Reyes's mine in the Sierra Madres, feeding the mules grain, so he wouldn't have to stop and graze them. Then along the way they would stash feed for their use on the trip out. No way to keep all this secret, but he planned for the swiftness of his strike in and out to be too fast for outlaws to get their forces ready and set up an ambush.

"I saw your friend, Amantha, this past week," Buffie said, standing by the porch post and looking toward the small lake, "when I took John to the train."

"She at the station?"

"No, I went out to the ranch. We didn't make her father's funeral and I wanted to tell her how sorry I was about that."

"She doing all right?"

"Oh, I think so, she did cancel her wedding engagement."

"Oh."

Buffie turned and sat on the railing, stretching her lace-up high-top shoes out before her. She patted on the tops of her legs under the blue material. "You have a way of breaking hearts. But you knew that?"

"I never promised her anything but the return ride home."

Buffie pushed her light brown, curled hair back and shook her head at him like a knowing mother—despite the closeness in their age. "Face it, after a few good men, the ranks get thinner."

"You know my situation."

She agreed. "Yes, I can recall that shouting Ferd Abbott screaming right out there that we were hiding a known killer. How he was having us all arrested for shielding you."

"John wasn't here then, either?"

"No, but I was so tired of that man's threats. So I shot that blasted shotgun that's inside the door over Mr. Abbott's head and his horse bucked him off."

They both laughed. Then Slocum looked up and spotted a paint pony coming out of the greasewood desert with a hatless rider.

"The lover has arrived." Slocum, still laughing over her episode with Abbotts, stood up and thanked her. "John's a lucky man to have such a gracious wife."

"You think on what I said."

"Buffie, there's no other way."

"Think about it."

"I will," he said and stepped off the porch to go meet his man.

Before sunup, they left the pens and buildings, three miles south of the big springs.

"Where in the hell is that pretty, short woman you had cook for us last time?" Posey demanded above the braying jackasses and noise of breaking camp.

"She left me to marry an Englishman."

"Gawdamn that was a bad deal. That old Mexican that you've got hired must fart in the food he cooks for us."

"No time now. We've got to move."

"A damn army moves on its belly, and mine ain't feeling good eating his crap."

"Posey!"

"All right, but I told you the damn truth," Posey shouted after him.

Slocum ran to help Charlie Stone, who had a mule having a fit. The bearded skinner was being half drug on his toes by the runaway jackass, and it took both men on the lead rope to tuck his head under and roll him down in the dust. Stone rushed over before the mule could start to get up and sat on his head. There, out of wind, he parked atop the animal and rolled a cigarette.

"You sum bitch, you'll learn. But from here it looks like it'll be hard making a believer out of you."

Forty mules and every train had its own share of jinxed ones. These packers had each one named. They knew them and their tricks well, except for the new ones added to their string. Additions were always bad; that's why the last guy sold them, and the better they looked the wilder they usually came.

Only the trustworthy ones were loaded with feed and supplies. Roman Jones, twenty miles into Mexico, was going to swing east to a small *rancheria* where he knew the owner. There he would leave two mule loads of feed and supplies they might need on the return trip. In the hills, it could be a good place for an ambush or a place to ambush any pursuers.

Slocum felt good in the soft predawn, heading south with his crew and the mules. His saddlebags contained ten sticks of loaded explosives. Dynamite with five-minute cords on each one that he could cut shorter if necessary. Besides he packed two more crates if he needed more fire power.

Each man and scout carried a pistol, some carried two, a hundred rounds of ammo, and a rifle with a hundred brass cartridges for them. Maybe overkill, but whatever they turned at him, he wanted to turn back. Three scouts rode out in front and two would watch the back trail when they got going. It was possible to make over fifty miles a day with this sort of teamwork.

Noontime, Roman Jones and Silver Bell rode east. They promised to rejoin the crew after dark at Coyote Wash. The short Apache knew the way well and Jones felt once his mules were unloaded, they would make lots of tracks to catch up. So when they parted Slocum swung up in the saddle and they left, southward-bound in a long trot. A bulk of the cranky ones were coming around, and forced by their counterparts, they learned it was better to be part of the string than to try to bolt it.

Aside from the dust they raised that Slocum scowled at—twisted in the saddle looking back—they were making good time. If Reyes had the loads ready, they could be out of the mine and on the road in a few hours. He wanted that for sure. Though he knew none of the employees, he trusted no one who worked for the man. His record of robberies was too long. Someone inside that mine was telling the criminals when and where to strike and no doubt sharing in their rich takes. Not one of the last three shipments made it.

Complete ambushes. No witnesses were alive was how Reyes described the robberies. Even the federales could only say they were a tough bunch and left little clues. Also, to do that so successfully they needed inside information. This time he hoped to surprise them and then fly away if his plan worked.

He couldn't forget Posey's complaint about the only other team member. The old man had been a trail drive cook, he said. Monticello was his name, and Slocum had seen him once or twice that morning riding along with the string since they broke camp.

Monticello passed out jerky or gruel—the corn and brown sugar mix that the vaqueros packed with them. Whatever they wanted to eat was washed own with canteen water that was from Slaughter's windmill, so the bad stuff was ahead. The liquid from Coyote Wash wouldn't be that sweet when they drank it on the second day. Of course, half the men drank whiskey, so what was worse. Lucky for Slocum the temperature was only in the nineties—in another thirty days it would soar in the hundreds.

Mules, men, and hoses were done in when they set up picket lines in the marshy bottoms of Coyote Wash. Cienga Coyote was the Spanish name. How in the middle of a hundred miles of alkali and brittle greasewood was one broad wash seeping precious water and holding enough for fowl-like ducks to stay there year-round. The tules grew profusely in the wash, and always there was enough water for stock. The mules were cooled down, then watered and finally fed corn and oats with nose bags.

Slocum checked on Monticello. The old man acted like he knew his business. He had brought a side of meat to cook, kept it cool all day under a wet canvas. Slocum felt it was the best he could expect and went to talk to his Apache flankers, who had ridden in only minutes before.

"Nothing out there," Caychem said, and the others agreed.

"Day one. They didn't have time. I'd bet money there was someone visiting his relatives on the Slaughter ranch that rode a

horse half to death to Fronteras in the last few days to tell someone like Hernandez that we had a mule train poised on the border."

"He wouldn't ambush us without a load?" Curly asked.

"They would steal their grandmother's gold tooth if they
could get away with it." The scouts laughed at his comments.

"Tomorrow will we go to San Delmar or the Montez Ran-
cho?" Caychem asked.

"If you were me, where would you go?"

"The mission. The padres would not tell anyone what we do,"
the youngest Apache, Tom, said.

"Fine. There is enough water there for this outfit?"

"Plenty, then we go up that north trail from there into the
Madres?" Caychem asked.

"Why?" Slocum wondered what his man was getting at about
their route.

"I will go tonight and be sure there is no one in that pass. You
see smoke you know there are some. Two smokes you go around."

"Good idea. Be damn careful."

"Someone is coming." The scouts stood up to try to see in the
crimson sunset. Sounds of hooves drumming the ground came
from the north.

"It's Silver Bell and Roman," Slocum said. "They made good
time."

The scouts agreed and dropped back down on their haunches.

"Curly, you will take the lead in the morning. You three spread
out and be sure we have no surprises."

The Apaches nodded. Caychem stood up to leave.

"Get some food, too," Slocum said after Caychem.

His man acted like he heard him, so Slocum turned back to the
others. "You have any doubts, come get me."

"Where did they attack the other pack trains?" Curly asked.

"Once up close to the border. Once in the Madres, only a few
miles from the mine, and the last one they think they did somewhere out here. No one found much left to tell them."

"What about the mules?"

Slocum frowned at the scout. "Maybe they ate them."

"Mules will go home."

"Oh, you're saying if you turn them loose, they'll head for
where they use to live, huh?"

Curly nodded.

"Be damned if I know, but it's good to know."

"These mules turned loose would go back to Arizona unless they were caught and penned."

"Good question. I may ask Reyes when I see him."

The next day passed uneventfully, save the contrariness of the mules and the usual frays that they presented to the packers. Things were too smooth for Slocum when in late afternoon they swung in on the small mission settlement.

He raised his eyes toward the foothills that butted against the plots of irrigated fields of beans and corn. Somewhere up there Caychem was scouting the way. Slocum felt better knowing that he had someone looking out for it all.

In blazing orange from the sunset above the shorter range, were towered over by the purple, lofty Sierra Madres. Without a hitch, they would be at Reyes's mine in late afternoon the next day. *Good*.

The padre, Father Simon, came and shook his hand to welcome him to the mission.

"Such fine mules," the priest said walking beside him.

"Expensive too," Slocum said.

"I would think so. You must have a very important task to accomplish."

"Yes, we do. We will be on our way in the early hours, and we appreciate your people letting us water and stay here tonight."

"No problem, we are the place for the weary traveler."

Slocum looked around to be sure no one would overhear his next question. "Tell me, did the pack trains from the Reyes mine come through here?"

"No."

"I guess they went north, when they dropped out of the foothills."

"A survivor of the last robbery was brought here. He was very badly wounded and only lived for a short while."

"Did he say anything?"

Father looked at his sandals and at the off-white ground and nodded. "He said, 'Those bandits knew our way.' "

"No names, descriptions, nothing else?"

"No."

"Thank you, I feared that someone at the mine must be feeding the bandits the information."

"Any way I can assist you?"

"No, Father, we have enough help."

"I see you have several Indios with you." He motioned to the Apaches squatted down to smoke and wait for supper.

"Former army scouts. They'll hurt no one."

"I was not concerned. Only making note of them. You sound educated. Most train masters are of a more earthy cut."

"Thanks, but I'm one of them."

"Indeed, I can see that, but it is nice to talk English with someone civilized for a change."

He parted with the priest after offering for him to join his crew for supper, though he had to agree with Posey's first observation that after Myra's cooking this Monticello was not the best.

His cook finally rang the dinner bell and everyone shuffled for the line. Sundown cast a crimson light over the church's reddish plaster and the palm trees looked dipped in blood. Slocum waited for the others to fill their plates, considering what he should do next. Then he heard a horse and spotted Caychem riding in.

"Well, is the way clear?" he asked the tired-looking Apache.

"No problem, but there are two camps in the hills."

Slocum dropped his head and sighed. "Who are they?"

"One I think must be Hernandez. The other is that hombre Phillipe."

"Two camps?" He shook his head. One set of bandits was enough; two would be hard to dodge. "The priest said a wounded packer from the last robbery spoke before he died about them having information from inside the mine. No names."

"These bandits went back and forth freely to the cantinas where the miners drank at night."

"Whiskey talks."

Caychem nodded.

"Then they'll let us in, but not out, huh?"

"Yes." Slocum began thinking aloud. "If we had a barrel of whiskey for each camp and got them drunk tomorrow night, maybe we could ride by them and get on our way to the border before they knew about it."

"Where is the whiskey?" Caychem asked with a smile.

"Roman Jones," Slocum called to the packer.

"Hey, you're back," the packer said to the scout between bites from his plate when he walked over. "What's wrong?"

"A man needed two barrels of whiskey, where would he get it?"

"Some bootlegger, they're set up all over."

"We need two barrels."

"I'll find you two after I finish eating. Soon enough?"

"Fine. You go eat some supper, then we'll find two burros to deliver them with."

"Plenty of them around," Caychem said and went to the cooking area.

Slocum followed him. Deliver the whiskey to the outlaws and then sweep out of the Madres with his train. It might give them enough of a lead to escape any plans to rob his outfit.

The matter of timing was all important. Two bands of outlaws were set up to get the next shipment. Both could learn all they wanted about gold shipments by plying the miners with drinks at night. His job was to disable the outlaws, then run like hell.

The border still lay two and half hard days' ride north, and even on the U.S. side, they could worry about outfits like the Clantons trying to hold them up between the border and Silver City. Slocum set up a plan to use guards around the mules and camp for the night—too close to his destination to have any problems.

Past midnight, Jones woke him up and pointed to two barrels. "Cost you fifty bucks."

"Cheap enough."

"If I'd had more time to dicker I'd got them for thirty-five." He handed Slocum the balance of the money he'd sent with him.

"Cheap enough, anyway. Thanks, get some sleep."

"I will."

Slocum rolled over and went back to slumber land.

Caychem had two burros captured before sunup when the mules began braying and kicking up their heels. He also had traded for two small pack saddles.

"You and Silver Bell this afternoon drive a whiskey-loaded burro into each of the camps," Slocum told his head scout. "We'll be loaded up and coming out by dark. I want to make the well at Casa Nova by midnight."

Caychem nodded. "Not come back this way."

"Let them think that we will, huh?"

A sly smile in the corners of his mouth. "You are going to tell them that at the mine?"

"Yes, that we're going out by San Del Mar."

Everything in order, Slocum took his horse and headed for the mine to prepare things. Reyes should be there by this time. Probably walked the soles off his fancy white dog leather shoes by this time. Horse and mules were making the long hard days fine. But the real test would come when they were loaded down with three hundred to three fifty pounds of gold ore apiece.

And a week's flight to Silver City. The first person Slocum saw when he rode up to the rifle-toting guard for a short conversation about his pack train coming behind him was Reyes in his snap brim panama hat and white clothing. He looked beside himself.

"Oh, where is the train?" The little man searched around like they were lost.

Slocum dropped from the saddle heavily and his spurs clinked. "Easy, they are coming."

"Oh." The man mopped his face on a white kerchief. "There is so much resting on this shipment."

"I know. You ever see any of those mules around here from the last robbery?"

"Why would they be here?"

Slocum led the horse toward the office building. "Cause mules go home."

"I don't think so. Ask David the mine manager. You think you can get this one out?"

"I'll do everything possible to get it to the smelter."

"Good—good—have you seen any bandits?"

"Just two bands."

"Two bands—oh, my God. Two?"

Slocum nodded and looked up at the American that walked out.

"You must be Slocum I've heard so much about. David Simmons is my name."

"Nice to meet you. I suppose everything is ready?" Slocum asked.

"Oh, yes," Reyes said. "We've been ready for days."

"Guess your mules and men will be tired after the long trip down here?"

"I suppose so," Slocum said, not entirely trusting the reddish-haired mine manager with his freckles. No one he could completely trust at this point.

"I will have the barracks cleaned out for your men, and we have ample corrals for the stock. I'll be sure there is plenty of fodder in the bunkers."

"Thanks," Slocum said. Fodder to feed them his butt. Those mules would be grain fed. "Good, show me the ore and how you have it ready."

"This way," Simmons said and Reyes nodded in approval, traipsing along beside Slocum.

The mine superintendent unlocked a large padlock on the thick door of a structure at the side of the office and shoved it in. Slocum stepped past him. The room was piled high with bulging white sacks.

"Fifty pounds in each one," Simmons said.

Slocum nodded in approval. "Very good."

"Of course, you couldn't get all of this in one trip."

"No, not in one." Slocum felt certain he could put a big dent in the storeroom supply though.

"Where is your train coming from today?" Simmons asked.

"San Del Mar."

"Nice easy trail up here and back out of here."

Slocum agreed. *Think what you want, brother. We'll have those loaded and be on our way in short time*—today.

"What do you think about bandits?" Reyes asked quietly.

"In Mexico? Several," Slocum said, wondering how his whiskey plot was working. The train would arrive in a few hours.

"From San Del Mar, it'll be dark before your mule train gets here, won't it?" Simmons asked.

"Probably," Slocum said and grinned at Reyes. "How is our friend in Fronteras?"

"Oh, quite well. Quite well. She sent her love."

"When you return tell her I sent mine."

"Oh, I am so nervous about this shipment."

"Rest easy, my friend, the gold will get through this time."

"Are the federales helping you?" Simmons asked.

Slocum laughed. "Their ranks are so full of convicts I wouldn't trust them with a nickel."

"My opinion exactly."

"It is a sad day when a country's army is full of outlaws too," Reyes said.

"No one else wants to fight the Yaquis."

Slocum agreed. He wasn't sure whether this man Simmons could be trusted or not. Never mind, inside of two hours his outfit would be headed north in a lightning-like strike.

"Let us go find some lunch," Simmons offered, and they both agreed. Though Reyes doubted he could eat.

They were in the middle of their meal when the noise of the pack train arriving made Simmons bolt upright and run to look.

"The train is here already—no way that they came from Del Mar in that time."

Slocum nodded and continued eating. "Have your men help load the mules, we will leave here in one hour."

"I can't believe this—"

With a peeved look after the man going out the door, Slocum said, "Lots more won't believe it either."

"You've shocked Simmons," Reyes said, holding up his goblet of wine and acting more relaxed. "I feel much better."

"Why, because we shocked him?"

"Partially and partially because I strongly believe you know what in the hell you're doing."

Slocum nodded and finished his sliced beef, chewing on the tender cut slowly. "I sure hope so."

21

One thirty on Reyes's gold Swiss watch, Roman Jones gave the shout and the sweat-soaked packers and Indian scouts left the Reyes Mine in a long trot.

"If I had not seen this in action, I'd have called you a liar. No one even suspected you'd be here today, and you sure never even told us." Simmons shook his head, watching the mules line out.

"Sorry," Slocum said. "One word dropped to an outlaw could cost these men their lives. I trust no one. My job is get this ore to the smelter in Silver City."

"Impressive." Simmons shook his head. "You can't make it this way, we better shut down; we'll never get any gold out of these mountains."

"God be with you," Reyes said and clapped him on the arm.

"You can meet Roman Jones up there," Slocum said to Reyes. "He'll be in charge."

"What about you?"

"I'll be seeing you."

"Good," the man in the white suit said and shook his hand.

The push to the wells was a hard descent out of the cooler heights of the Madres Steep, narrow trails where the panniers rubbed on the side walls of the mountain face and the other side hung over a thousand-foot or more sheer cliff. The trip tested the men's nerves, and the Apache scouts on foot in only loincloths darted in and out of tall cracks in the gray and tan-faced rocks to be certain no ambush lurked for them.

They reached a narrow valley and paused to water the stock in the small silver stream. Slocum looked up and saw Caychem and the boy returning.

The scouts reined up their horses and grinned big. "We sold the keg to Hernandez's men for ten dollars."

"What about Phillipe's bunch?"

"They stole it from us."

"Plenty of drunk bandits."

"Oh yes, but I think someone rode into Phillipe's camp after we left."

"Come from the mine?" Slocum asked.

"From that direction."

"You see them?"

"We were too high up the trail to see them."

"You did wonderful. We make it to the springs by tonight, we can ride by John Slaughter's house tomorrow night. None of these bandits can ever catch us."

Mules watered, the men chewed on jerky and cussed the bang tails to get going again. Time to move on. In a few more hours, they would hit the village and camp for the night. Slocum knew mounting his horse that man and beast would be ready for that time and place.

Caychem and Curly scouted the small cluster of hovels and returned to report to him.

"There are some bad hombres in the cantina," Curly said, and they gathered off the trail for a conference.

"Maybe seven or eight," Caychem said.

"Not locals."

Both scouts shook their heads in the twilight.

"No, these are pistoleros and tough."

"How many innocent people are in this cantina?" Slocum asked. "If it was only banditos we could blow it up."

"Maybe some *putas* and bartenders. They ran all the locals away."

"That won't work. We better take them out."

"How?"

"Get them separated and one by one get them."

Caychem smiled. "Paint them?"

"Not this time. Take their clothes and guns and horses."

"Now?"

"Yes, I'll tell Roman what we're going to do. Get two more scouts."

Slocum booted his horse into a short lope to overtake the leader. When he caught up to Jones, he told him to slow the train down and they'd take out the bandits.

Roman agreed, and Slocum loped off with four Apaches.

At the village in the gathering darkness, Slocum assigned Silver Bell to get the bandits' horses from out in front as quietly as he could. Slocum took the others and led them to the side of the cantina where several open windows he felt were for the women's rooms.

Like a thief in the night, Caychem climbed in the first one and Tom followed. A short scream soon cut off and then some struggling. Slocum came in the window, and Tom dragged over the small *puta*, one hand over her mouth, the other around her chest under her small breasts. The only light in the room was the flickering candle at her shrine.

"We won't hurt you," Slocum hissed in Spanish. "I will pay you five pesos for each bandito you bring back here."

He motioned for Tom to let up on her mouth.

She gasped for her breath. "They will kill me."

"They will never know."

"I am scared."

"Then get the other girls out of the building and the bartender and I'll blow it up."

"Where will I work then?"

"Go get me another bandit."

She agreed, moved over, and put on a robe.

"No tricks," Slocum warned her as she went through the blanket door and up the hallway.

The first outlaw was already stripped of his clothes and boots, tied, gagged, and lying face down on the floor.

"Oh, him," the *puta* said—her words put them all against the wall. Everyone held their breath, and when she came in, Caychem coldcocked the bandit over the head.

"How many more are up there?"

"Three."

"Where are the others?" he asked in a whisper.

"With the other girls, I guess."

"Stay here," Slocum told her. He didn't need to tell the Apaches what to do to those in the other rooms. He went up the hall gun in hand.

When he stepped in the barroom, he nodded to the bartender and pointed his gun at the three sitting at the table. "Hands high."

"Who are you?" the black-bearded one asked.

"Shuck them guns and your clothes."

"Huh?"

"Get them guns out slow like. I've got an itchy finger."

He moved in and swept the weapons away. "Now take off all your clothes."

"Who the hell are you—"

"You want to be dead naked or what?"

"I'm undressing, but if I ever catch you—" He blinked hard when the other three pistoleros were shoved into the barroom, hands tied and naked as jaybirds.

"What's your name?" Slocum asked, using his gun barrel for an indicator pointed at the man.

"Benito Chavez."

"Tell your boss, Hernandez, that his trick didn't work."

"Who said I worked for Hernandez?"

"Tell him and quite stalling."

The *putas* dressed in robes stood along the wall, meekly watching Slocum's plan unfold. The three finally were undressed, had their hands tied behind their backs, and were driven outside.

"Start walking," Slocum said and pointed south into the star-lighted night. "You come back here again, I'll kill you. Curly, you keep them walking until they get over the hills."

"He's an Apache, hombres," Slocum said after them. "You try anything he'll kill so quick you'll never even feel the knife slice your throat."

"But we're naked!"

"So was Adam. Curly, they ain't worth nothing to me."

The Apache nodded and forced his horse up to crowd them so they had to hurry and limp on the sharp things under their bare feet.

The next day, the temperature soared, but they still made good time. Noontime, they reached the small *rancheria* where Roman had stashed the grain. Mules were watered and fed—Slocum knew for certain then they would be at Slaughter's south pens shortly after sundown.

John rode down to the camp that evening with a good bottle of whiskey.

"Man, oh, man, you are making lots of news. Every newspaper in the country is covering this train. Word's the Yaquis have attacked you twice to steal the gold in one paper I saw."

"We haven't seen a Yaqui all the way. Where're these papers getting all this news?"

"Some reporter claims he interviewed you."

"In his dreams, maybe. I haven't talked to any reporter or newsman."

"Exciting stories, anyway."

"It also means I can't ride into Silver City."

"I hadn't thought about that. Buffie's buddy Abbott will be there. Shame that her aim hadn't been lower. Damn it, I brought two glasses and a bottle. Let's go somewhere and have a drink."

Slocum caught his horse's reins and held him still. "Get down. We've got two kegs we can sit on right here."

"Ah, furniture," Slaughter said and laughed.

Drinks poured, the rancher dropped his elbows on his spread out legs and shook his head. "I come to tell you, you have one more to get by—old man Clanton's bunch. You won't ever get up the San Pedro Valley north of here, without them being on you like hornets."

"I appreciate that."

"They been riding by here for several days in threes and fours. He must have every hard case hired from here to Fort Worth."

"Guess I could go around the Chiricuhuas on the west. Be some out of my way, but at Bowie I could request a military escort to Silver City."

Slaughter laughed out loud. "Good tactics of war. Splendid, let's have another drink to that."

"Pour away. I'm going to send for Roman Jones and Caychem. They'll have to take it the last of the way."

With his two leaders called in, Slocum explained to them about the newspaper articles, what that meant, and how they'd have to take the train on to Silver City after they got to Fort Bowie.

"Where we going to stay up there?" Jones asked.

"Myra Downing's tomorrow. She should have enough good hay for the mules. Then the next day move up to the Grant ranch. We can stay there I'm certain, while you go over and get a military guard to take you to the smelters."

"We'll go over the Mules Shoes and down into the Sulfur Springs Valley?"

"Like we came down here to get Amantha Grant."

"Beat having a gunfight with the Clantons," Roman said and let John pour some whiskey in his tin cup.

"I've got some old horses," Slaughter said. "What if we used them for a decoy and let that bunch chase a few of us up the valley."

"Sure throw them off," Roman said.

"I'll have a half dozen of my boys ready to go at daybreak," John said.

"I've got my saddlebags full of dynamite. We get them to chase us we can throw it down and let them have it."

"Hell, I never would have thought about doing that," Slaughter said. "Maybe I'll get even with them damn rustlers."

Four Mexican boys in their late teens, no doubt good riders, the black man John T., Slaughter, and John's foreman, Rafaele, started north from the ranch, making lots of dust. Slocum armed Slaughter, John T., and Rafaele with dynamite, explaining how to light and toss it.

"Five minutes, two minutes," he said, as if he'd cut the cord in half. Even in a trot the dust the old broodmares and stiff ranch horses made would have been visible for miles.

Some of the individual animals began to drop out and Slocum worried they might be uncovered as hoaxes. But out of the side canyon chocked in junipers came four riders blasting away.

Rafaele lit a charge and then sent his own horse racing into the cloud of dust. Slocum was right behind him. He looked back in time to see the explosion go off behind the riders. Their horses went crazy and raced away uncontrollable at the onset and one went to bucking his rider. Slocum headed for the next rise to look ahead.

He watched John T. fling a stick in the brushy draw, then ride for the herd. The blast blew foliage and dust high in the air, sending the concealed horses and riders in all directions.

Slocum felt certain the Clantons wanted no more. Besides, they realized they had been tricked by this time—meanwhile, Slocum knew the pack train was going over the Mule Shoes and must be at Sutter's ranch by this time.

The Slaughter Ranch crew was crying from laughing so hard.

"Dad buckskin him had his tail glued to his ass and could ah won the Kentucky Derby," John T. broke up laughing. "Dat—dat-damn outlaw's eyes was big as silver dollars and him ah hanging on for dear life."

Slocum shook their hands and thanked them.

"Come back, we'll have more fun," Slaughter said.

Slocum used the most direct way to cross the Chiricuhuas and reached Myra's place after dark. The mules were all in her lots, and Silver Bell armed with a rifle met him.

"No trouble?"

"No trouble. That Myra is looking for you."

Slocum looked up at the house. There were lights on. "I'll go see what she wants."

"Posey say, we finally eat something good tonight."

"I'll bet you did." He booted the tired pony uphill.

The youth clapped his horse on the butt when he rode by him. *The place was guarded—Roman knew they weren't out of danger even here. Good.*

Slocum dropped out of the saddle at the gate, found his sea legs, and stood there for a moment. Nodding hard, he watched her get out of the rocker.

"I didn't marry the damn Englishman they sent me."

"Shame, he might of had you drinking tea."

"Roman offered me a job."

"Good."

"You ain't asking what he wants me to do?"

"Cook, so Posey won't complain."

"You care?"

He dropped his butt down to the edge of the porch. "Do what you have to do."

"You don't care then?"

"No, but I ain't slept either. I could crawl up here and sleep a few hours, I might make decent company."

"You are done in?"

Using his hands for pillow, he sprawled on the porch flooring and closed his eyes.

The last thing he recalled was her saying, "I'll get you a blanket."

22

Slocum had his dusty boots on the table and was leaned back in the chair half asleep. Day three at Mayletta's (the German still wasn't back from Mexico City) and except for one pestering fly, his afternoon had gone exactly as he desired it—calm and peaceful. Half asleep, he opened one eye when a barefoot boy rushed in calling his name.

"Senor Slocum?"

He dropped his boots down with a clunk of his spurs and announced, "That's me."

"I have a message for you."

"Good, who sent it?"

"I don't know his name. He paid me to bring it to you."

Slocum sat upright in the chair. "What's this hombre look like gave it to you?"

"He was a vaquero passing through."

"No pistolero?"

"No senor, he was a caballero."

He opened the envelope. The writing was that of a woman's fine penmanship.

Dear Slocum,

I am sorry you can't come dance at my wedding, but you explained all that last week. You would really like Tom. No cowboy, but very athletic. He'll fit in here I am certain.

Word came to me yesterday that Ryhmer and Larson were staying in a place called Los Negas. I don't know where that is. You don't need to go after them for me, but you asked that I inform you if I heard anything.

Be careful, you will always be my hero.

Amantha Grant

"Where are you going in the heat of the day?" Mayletta asked, coming in the room and seeing him on his feet.

"Taking a little side trip down to Los Negras."

"What is down there? I never hear of that place."

"Two outlaws who killed a man across the border."

She made a pained face. "Why leave here? You have plenty whiskey and pussy here."

"Business."

She waved away the notion with her brown hands. "Business, what is that? He went to Mexico City six weeks ago and business must have ate him."

Slocum agreed. "He's sure had plenty of time to go there and come back." She narrowed her long, dark lashes. "Maybe this will be all mine?"

"Don't count on it."

"It could be. I have all the money and keys."

He hugged her shoulder. "He knows you're a good woman."

"When will you be back?"

"Days or weeks."

A look of impatience swept her face. "Don't stay long away too long. I will miss you."

"Me, too." He set out for the livery. The Los Negras he knew about was in the mountains. Maybe a two-day ride away. Wouldn't those two be surprised to see him?

He brought the strawberry roan over to the cantina to load up his gear. The stout bulldog mountain horse would be a fine choice for his trip. All rested, he would be a little spunky, but that would help—the day and a half across the desert would be boring.

Saddlebags and bedroll tied on, he kissed Mayletta and stepped in the saddle.

"I may be gone from this godforsaken place if you stay away too long, hombre," she threatened after him.

He waved that he heard her and let the roan jig walk for the east. A hot blast of wind struck his face. The next thirty-six hours would be miserable as being in a bakery oven, except late at night.

Why didn't he wait for sundown to leave? He shook hs head. Sometimes he did things the hard way.

23

The drum of the three horses' hooves, the creak of saddle leather in Slocum's ear. Rasping breathing of the animals, he pushed them hard, looking back over his shoulder, his mind filled with dread. His pursuers were still coming.

They crossed a wide dry wash and topped the other side. He wouldn't have feared the outcome of this pending collision if he'd been alone. But the two prisoners were like a heavy millstone chained around his neck—neither mobile nor cooperative. The notion of a standoff with an army made his guts churn.

By this time, Ryhmer must have figured out his concern. "Give us both a gun."

He shook his head, reined up on the rise to let the horses breath and catch their breath.

"I might give you to them. I ain't giving either of you a gun."

"Who do you figure they are?"

"Some bandits heard about all the money you two stole."

"Give 'em the damn money." Ryhmer looked to the tight-lipped Larson for assurance, who agreed with a bob of his head.

"I ain't much to yield to their kind." The small range of hills to Slocum's right looked like the place they needed to be for any standoff.

"There's a time to be stubborn and a time to give in, too," Ryhmer said. "Looks like they've got all the guns."

"We're going to break for them hills. You better spur them horses or your asses will be the first ones they get. I'll leave you for cannon fodder."

They charged for the hills, and Slocum decided the outlaws knew their only chance to maybe live to see the border was ride hard and they did. In the canyon, he saw the way would be too rough for horses and dropped out of the saddle. He unlocked them, then chained the pair together.

"Start up that mountain. One wrong move and you'll be dead. That means the other guy is chained to your dead body. Think on on it." He could hear the clatter of oncoming horses and the shouts of their riders entering the canyon as they came up.

He jerked the Winchester out of the boot, cut loose his bedroll with his knife and let it fall. Then he slashed the leather ties that held the saddlebags, and after a quick glance back, he started climbing for the house-sized boulder up the slope, the bags on his shoulder. The canyon floor would soon swell with riders. They needed to be to the pass high above them.

Ahead, he could see the pair stumbling and sliding on the black volcanic rocks. But they were halfway to the divide. Sharp edges could cut like a knife. His boot soles crunched on the ages-old, splinted lava flow. He caught the two near a large massive black block and motioned for them to get behind it. His words were punctuated by shots from the mad melee of riders swarming around in the V-shaped canyon bottom.

Too far away for their pistols to do any harm, he stopped and took aim. The .44/40 shots reverbed off the sides of the hills. Horses screamed in pain and riders shouted they were hit. Several fled the the bottoms, and caught in the angry fire of his rifle, they rode out of sight. Some sought cover and returned pistol fire, but the range was far too great for any success.

Out of wind from the climb, both outlaws were seated on their butts, huffing for their wind.

"You're sure a crazy sum bitch," Ryhmer said at last. "Why, I'd bet there's thirty damn guns down there."

"You ever hear what the Apaches said about the Mexicans?" With the rifle resting against the side of the rock, Slocum looked away from his aim at the outlaw.

"No."

"We use rocks on the Mexicans. Save the bullets for the Americans."

"They'll surround us by dark."

Slocum nodded he heard him, then he snapped off two more shots. Both counted for casualties. "If they have anyone left."

"That guy that pays them ain't letting them run off."

"Who's that?" Slocum asked, thinking perhaps that Ryhmer knew more about them than he did.

"How the fuck should I know?"

"They came after the money that you two stole." Slocum slid fresh cartridges in the magazine and waited for the reply.

"We're going to die in these damn godforsaken hills. You know that?"

"They sure ain't the garden of eden," Slocum said and took three more well-aimed shots. Two out of three wasn't bad. So far he'd cut down a half dozen of the gang. Chances were good—they might decide they didn't want any more of his lead.

Then the real test would come. They'd be on foot when they tried to escape. It was thirty maybe forty miles to Slaughter's place. No water and a long way to any.

He pressed his cheek to the wood stock and half squinted his right eye. The one in the soiled white pancho dodging right and left with a pistol in his hand was leading the charge, waving the others on after him. The bead of the sight on his throat, Slocum squeezed the trigger.

The bullet struck him in the center of his face. At the force and impact, he threw his hands in the air and flew backwards. His stunned followers stopped and looked in dismay at his plight. The one on his right was struck in the chest by the next bullet. The other one on the left turned to go back in time to take his hot lead in the center of his back.

The outlaws had enough. The remaining ones mounted up and rode hard out of the canyon. Slocum wondered how far they would ride. Was it all a ploy to throw him off? If they were running away, would they reconsider and come back? Enough horses left down there to ride off on. But it might expose them to a trap.

A trickle of sweat from under the his hat band ran down his cheek. Both eyes stung with the invading salty fluid. What should he do next? Wait until dark, perhaps, and then slip off the hillside. No, he had a better Idea. Send one of the prisoners down there under his rifle sights. They might ride off once they were down there, taking a chance on him missing them. Might pick up a pistol that one of the bandits dropped. No matter, the situation amounted to a chance he must take.

He set down the rifle. "Ryhmer, I'm sending you down after two horses."

"Me?"

"Hold out your wrists." Slocum squatted down to unlock the padlock and then put the chain on both of Larson's. "Listen good. One trick and I'll put a bullet in you. My aim isn't bad. I've cut down several down there.

"Get the two horses and get back up here."

Ryhmer rose to his haunches. "What's in it for me?"

"It'll save you a forty-mile hike to San Bernadino Springs."

Ryhmer swiped his mouth on the back of his hand. "I never was one for much walking." Then he stood up as Slocum did and set out.

A long time lapsed. Aware that Larson was seated on his butt nearby, Slocum kept the rifle pointed at the black leather vest making his descent down the dim trail.

"You got three here," Ryhmer shouted back, passing the last chargers' bodies. "Damn good shooting. More of them down here." The killer stopped and looked back uphill at him. "You damn sure can shoot. Looks like a damn battlefield."

"Bring those horses and quit talking."

"I am. I am."

Slocum worried Ryhmer might use one of the animals for a shield, grab a pistol from one of the downed Mexicans, and then take a chance on riding off. The minutes clicked away. At last, his man caught their horses and began to lead them up the hill.

Wary of many things that could explode the situation, Slocum watched for any sign of reprisal—nothing, except for Ryhmer cussing the hesitant horses he led as their shoes clattered on the rocks, losing footing sometimes and scrambling to get more. Step by step he brought them up the canyon side.

Nothing moved. No one returned to fight. So far so good—but whoever sent them would be more determined the next time. He and his wards needed to get over the border and quickly.

When the out-of-breath Ryhmer reached the rock, Slocum quickly appraised the horses. They looked sound enough and rested some. He ordered them in the saddle, cuffed them, and mounted the roan. They went over the divide and half slid down the far side of the range. On the desert floor, he headed north in the sweltering heat of the afternoon. Slapped by oven-like blasts of wind, they rode in a long trot for the ranch. Both grumbling outlaws remained silent as the day swept by them, engulfed in shimmering heat waves and the bitter dust churned up by their own horses' hooves.

Slocum turned in the saddle. His eyes burned like an iron-wood fire—hot and hard. His study of the horizon at their backs showed nothing in the azure sky. Had he beat off his opposition? Something niggled him. They weren't through. They weren't at the ranch—yet. He could only hope that his dulled wits were better than theirs.

No saliva to draw in his mouth—he wondered if he would even live to see John again himself. Blinking his dry eyes didn't help either. They felt sore as fire pits. Waves of anxiety swept over him like the fiery winds that scorched their faces. What would the pair try next? He knew they laid in waiting for him to make a mistake they could pounce upon and get away.

Still, his bluff had held them in check this long. If the heat weakened him enough and they saw their chance—his dehydrated carcass would become buzzard bait. He fought the drowsy feelings and shifted his weight in the saddle, hoping to find some new energy. None came.

"You're—" Ryhmer cleared his throat but his voice still sounded rusted. "You're a strange sum bitch, Slocum. You could have already shot me and Larson and took our heads in a tow sack back to the damn Arizona law."

"So?" He fought his lead weight eyelids wanting to close forever.

"That's revenge. I want justice for what you did to her."

"I don't see the sense."

"And I couldn't show you. Trust me, you'll pay for your crime."

"You saying we'll stand trial for raping her?"

Slocum focused on the heat distorted horizon. "No, but for the murder and robbery of Albert Grant, you'll swing from the scaffold."

"Why don't you just shoot us and get it over with then?"

Slocum shook his dull head and booted the roan back into a trot. *Poor horse, this trip might finish him forever.* He twisted in the saddle. No dust, but that didn't mean anything. When word got back that he'd shot up their gang, there would be more sent after them. Time, distance, and their condition all entered into this race. Heat too was a big factor—it had been sapping away at his strength. Nothing left in their canteens.

"Hey!" Ryhmer shouted as the tug on the lead sent Slocum's hand for his gun butt. "Larson passed out."

The outlaw had fallen from the saddle, but his cuffed arm was still holding him up. Larson's horse had shied at his initial fall, but by then stood spraddle-legged and wearily snorted in the dust.

Slocum dropped the reins and with care unlocked the padlock. Released, the unconscious outlaw slumped to the ground. After a quick check of Ryhmer, who was leaning on his saddle horn and looked as done in as well, he bent over to hoist the prisoner over the saddle.

The effort required three tries. He bound the man belly down over his horse, and when he finished, he wondered if he had the strength left to remount the roan. His second try, he swung his leg over and into the stirrup.

How much further? No way to know anything, except they were headed right. The detour had confused him about how much more distance they must cover. Another while, he paused to let the horses rest.

"Uncuff me," Ryhmer begged. "I'm so damn dizzy. I may fall out of this saddle any minute."

He booted the dull acting roan over to him and undid the lock, then secured Ryhmer's hands together. Without wasting any of his strength on a warning, he shared a tough look at the man. Ryhmer needed to know he was still in charge and would kill him. A toss of his head and he rode north again, leading the two horses.

Hours turned into more plodding drudgery. Then when the lead rope jerked in his hand, he heard something and turned to see that Ryhmer had fallen out of the saddle and lay facedown in the dirt. *Sum bitch. Trick or for real?*

24

It was dark. Slocum tried to wake up. Someone was laughing. Taunting laughter. Not Larson or Ryhmer's laughter.

"At last, we meet *mi* amigo."

Unsure who stood above him, the ring of the man's spur rowels was close enough to his face he could see them in the starlight.

"Where is the money?"

"What money?" Slocum was shocked by the hoarse sound of his own voice.

"Ah, everyone has been talking about the money."

A whiff of strong cigar smoke reached his nose and he could see the glow. "I don't have any money."

"We know that, we searched you. Where did you hide it, *mi* amigo?" The man shifted his weight where he squatted beside him and the spur rowels rang like silver bells.

"I don't know you."

"Victor Hernandez. Pardon my bad manners, but you have shot many of my men and the rest want to drag you behind a horse with a rope around your neck. Maybe you tell where the money is and I let you live."

"I don't have any money."

"Ah, hombre, we know that. But you have hid it somewhere."

Slocum shook his head, his lips so cracked they hurt him to even talk. "I don't know where it went. Ask them, they stole it."

"Those other two hombres are dead."

Dead? Where were they at? He was lying on the ground too weak to even rise up. In his shadowy mind, he could recall loading Ryhmer over the saddle and riding on past sundown. But he

170

couldn't recall falling off his own horse or how he got to this place on the ground.

"I have lost many men because of you, and my patience grows short."

"Can't help you—"

The quick kick from the man's boot toe drew an anguished cry of pain from deep in his raw throat. On Hernandez's command, strong arms lifted him, and soon he was lying on the rough boards of a cart. A woman was squeezing moisture in his mouth as they were thrown from side to side by the cart's movement.

Precious drops reached his swollen tongue and exploded in his oven-like mouth. Never before had the need for water felt so overwhelming.

"Not too fast, or you will die," she scolded. "The *patron* said you must live to tell him where you hid the money."

"Where do we go?"

"Off of the ranch."

"Whose?"

"Senor Slaughter's."

Damn. He had made it to the south end of the ranch after all. *So close and lost it*. Why was Hernandez moving? He didn't want to face John's wrath but there was little hope that anyone knew where he was at.

The whole irony was the bedroll with the money belts was deep in the canyon of the ambush he laid for Hernandez's men. If no one had found it, it was still there. In his own panic to escape, when he sent Ryhmer after the horses he'd even forgotten, slashing the ties off the saddle to get to his saddlebags full of cartridges. Survival could make one forget a lot of important things.

Her wet cloth felt like ice on his sore, fiery lips. On her knees rocking with the cart's side by side rolling, he could see she was young and attractive. Some camp follower with the bandits. But her Florence Nightingale care made him think he might live at least until Hernandez got through with him. Strange, how a man could want to survive longer so his hell on earth could continue another hour, another day—no matter how miserable the quality of his life would be—he still wanted to live that second tick longer. As if to give up was so dark and final.

The cart pulled by mules made much noise as the wooden wheels had no bearings, no springs for sure, and the two of them were tossed around by every bump. She would quickly recover, pour more liquid on the rag to wet it, and reapply it to his mouth.

Close to daylight, they rested the mules. Several riders came by and looked hard at him, then rode on. Too weak to sit up, he closed his eyes to shut out the morning's first light—too bright on the dry sand pits that contained his vision.

Hernandez sent his riders hither and yon to be on the lookout, to scout and be certain no one followed them. Slocum in his dull wisdom wondered who the hell the man feared. John Slaughter knew nothing about Slocum's intentions to use his ranch for anything. No one else would even know where he was at—nor give a rat's ass about his well-being. Maybe the widows of Sulfur Valley might. *Hell*—a bad bump jarred him. The place in the side of his rib cage where Hernandez had kicked him hurt. Not many places didn't ache over his entire body.

Somehow he had managed to outlive both outlaws. Crazy, they'd never stand trial, never do time in Yuma prison for raping her. He closed his eyes and tried to shut out the blazing sun. Where in the hell were they going? How long could he stall Hernandez? His life depended upon that issue. Once the outlaw knew the answer, he would be killed. Maybe on the end of a rope being drug by a stout horse. He wanted to grasp his own throat at the thought of it.

"What is wrong?" she asked, sounding concerned.

"I won't die on you. Give me more water."

They were going in the hills to some *rancheria*. Nothing made sense. Then he fainted again.

25

Slocum awoke in a hammock under the shade of a ramada. Palm fronds layered made up the roof over him, and several woman chattered like magpies nearby. He felt like a horse had rolled over on him. Every muscle in his body screamed, some twice. The woman in charge of his care brought a bowl and nodded at his being awake. She began to spoon the hot soup in his mouth, a few dribbles at a time.

"This will make you stronger," she promised.

Stronger for what? More interrogation. Some of Hernadez's torture. The salty flavor on his numb tongue made him decide that her dish came from chicken broth. *Damn, it tasted good.*

Where was Hernandez? His booming voice wasn't carrying across the camp ordering people around.

"Where—'s—the *patron*?" he managed to ask.

"He took the heads of those two men in a gunnysack to Tombstone for the reward," she said in a guarded voice.

Slocum nodded, then parted his lips for more soup. That simply meant he had more time before the torture began. In the company of the lovely Carmen, he didn't care. Her nursing was beginning to make him feel alive even with all the pain. What had happened to his shoulder? Must have been where he landed when he fell off the roan. Was the horse alive?

No way to know. Nothing he could do. If he was alive, the strawberry roan would go back to Myra's, if there were not fences or people to detain him. But he dismissed the notion and smiled at Carmen.

"Rest, *mi* amigo. The sleep will heal you."

He reached out and squeezed her hand. *"Gracias,"* he managed.

173

Two days passed, and he wondered if Hernandez had had trouble collecting the reward. Usually bounties were not immediately paid. Verification of the dead men had to be done and the money drawn from some account.

His bladder began to work and she assisted him to sit on the edge of the hammock so he could pee in a pot. Perhaps he would live. The lanolin she put carefully on his mouth, despite the strong sheep flavor, had softened his lips and stopped some of the hurting. Still, his strength's recovery evaded him. By the third day, he could sit up and feed himself. He could make a few steps using Carmen and another woman for support. Then, totally exhausted, he would lie back down and sleep for hours. Everything he did depleted him of any strength for a long while.

Day five and he had made it by himself twenty steps to the post that supported the corner of the ramada. There he could see this was the same *rancheria* that he had used as a supply stop for the Reyes's pack train. Where was the man and his wife that Roman Jones knew and trusted?

When he started back, his concerned nurse joined him. "You must no overdo it."

"Where is the man owns this place?"

She shook her head as if she couldn't tell him.

"Where is he?"

"Dead."

Then using her for support, he hobbled back to the bed. Obviously, Hernandez had taken it over for his own purposes. His own holster was gone. They'd taken his knives, the small amount of money he carried, everything. He realized there wasn't much he did have–but a pain-racked body and a lovely nurse.

Foolish for him to have gone after those two alone. He always well planned his missions in and out of Mexico. Did them in bold strokes. This one, he could not forget the sight of Larson with his erection white with lard ready to rape Jean. The sum bitch deserved more hell than he got.

"Anyone heard from the *patron*?" he asked her when she brought his supper.

"Yes, he heard about a gold mine shipment coming from the Madres. He missed the last one. Most of the men are going to join him over by the border where the pack train may cross."

"What's the name of the mine?"

"Reyes—I think."

Roman Jones's pack train. Damn, he hoped the man was ready for a strong attack. Nothing that he could do to save them—he closed his eyes, seated on the edge of the hammock.

"Is something wrong, Slo-cum?"

"Nothing we can do anything about."

She shrugged. "I was angry when he told me I must take care of you. I hated you very much. You killed my man in the fight in the canyon."

"Oh, I had no choice."

She reached in and made him a tortilla full of beans and meat as if impatient with his lack of progress on the food before him.

"I know that now."

He met her look head-on, her face only inches from his own. "You should leave this camp," he said.

"Where would I go?"

"Maybe across the border. I could get you a job."

"I can be a *puta* in Mexico."

He shook his head and waved away her concern. "I mean a real job."

"But"—she lowered her voice, being sure she would not be overheard by anyone—"He would not let me leave."

"We'll see." He went back to eating his burrito. How much time did he have left before Hernandez came back for him? That would be the question. He thanked her and went back to sleep. He still felt a flea could whip him in hand-to-hand combat.

He was walking good on the second day after they talked. Then he heard the shouts. "They return!"

Where was a gun? A pistol? Nothing. He hobbled back to the ramada. The women rushed out to greet the men, except Carmen, who stood and chewed on her knuckles at the edge of the ramada.

Seated on the edge of the hammock, he tried to shake the weakness from his brain. "What's wrong?"

"Many men did not ride back with him. The robbery must have gone wrong." She turned. "You will tell him where the money is, won't you?"

Slocum shook his head warily. "No way. Don't worry about me. They can only kill me once."

"They almost killed you last time. You are stupid as an ass." She stomped her foot and then stalked away.

He watched her go. Only thing he had to do was sit there and wait for his fate. Then something caught his eye. Piled in the corner of the ramada was his saddle and some other things. One was his dirty, sun-yellowed bedroll underneath, another saddle piled on top of it. Someone had fetched the bedding from the canyon, no doubt, and he had lain in a hammock only a few feet away from it all the time spent in Hernandez's camp.

Obviously no one considered it of much value. But he needed to give it to Carmen anyway—since he had no heirs and the end looked close.

Only thing she'd do with it would be to try to ransom him with it. Wrong idea to do that. Hernandez would kill him and then take the money belts away from her. How in the hell could he get her the money and not let that happen?

The women brought two wounded bandits to the ramada. Both men looked trail dirty, and one was unconscious. The other one had a hollow, blanched look. His lips formed an O and he moaned when they gently laid him in a hammock. Chances for them to live were about as good an odds as his own.

"They shot them up," one woman said, busy wiping the quiet one's face with a wet rag.

"I can see that."

"Several are dead."

"They must not have gotten the gold?"

She looked up from her chore at him with troubled dark eyes. "No gold."

He nodded and then dropped back on the hammock. *Good. Roman Jones had been prepared for them.* His attention on the sun-dried palm fronds that over laid the roof. *What next?*

Carmen brought his supper. When he awoke earlier, he had heard the ranting voice of Hernandez moving about in camp.

"Here is your food," she said sharply.

"You're angry?"

She looked away. The set to her long lashes told him she was upset. He used a corn tortilla to scoop up some mashed beans. "Why are you so angry?"

"You, for being so stubborn. Him for getting those men killed. Like he sent them after you, knowing you had to shoot them."

"Must be a time to hate."

"You will know what hate is—" She shook her head, rose, and fled the shelter.

"What is wrong with her?" they all asked in Spanish.

Slocum shook his head.

"Where is the money?"

The big man stood over Slocum. Hands on his hips. "Well, where did you hide it?"

"It was lost."

"Either you tell me where it is or you'll wish you were dead."

Slocum dismissed his threat with a "I don't know where it is."

"Your memory better get better." Hernandez turned on his heel and fled the tent.

"Oh," the woman close by said. "He will torture you bad, hombre."

Two burly men came and hustled him by the arms across the open campground. He was soon tied by his wrists over a high bar. They applied more pressure to pull him up until he stood on his toes. Then they grinned at each other, satisfied that they had been successful.

Slocum only hoped that the whole thing did not last too long. His mind went in and out of shadows as the weight of his body on his arms began to pull without any way to relieve them. Things looked serious for him—if he only could focus on what was happening in the camp.

Women were running everywhere. Men half-drunk were searching for their firearms. The camp was in total panic. The he saw the cause—Indians were attacking them.

War paint striped their faces and they were killing the men. They were Apaches, too. One rode up on a paint pony, reached out, and cut his rawhide binds. Slocum fell to his butt, expecting a hatchet to his head any moment.

"Get up, Slocum, we need to leave here."

What the hell? He looked up and saw Tom's face.

"Caychem said for me to get you on a horse and ride out at once."

"You can't load me on a horse—I can't even get up."

"Better hurry, him be mad I don't hurry." The younger Apache looked around wildly for an adversary.

On his hands and knees, Slocum started for the shelter.

"Where you going?" Tom shouted and then fired his pistol at one of the bandits trying to get away.

Two low running women soon reached Slocum.

"Hurry, we need to get you to shelter," Carmen said in his ear.

"The shade—"

"No, we can hide in the brush."

"No, the shade," he insisted as they each took an arm.

"Why?"

"The Apaches won't hurt you with me." He tossed his head toward the shade.

In disgust over his stubbornness, the two finally nodded at each other and put his arms over their necks. They half carried him to the shade in rapid fashion. Him seated, they both screamed when Caychem bounded off his horse.

"We must go."

Slocum shook his head. "I couldn't ride ten feet. Too weak."

The Apache nodded he understood, ran out, bounded on his horse, and rode away.

Still lots of fighting was going on. Shots being fired. War cries and thundering horses crossing and recrossing the campgrounds. Dust and confusion. More women came to cluster in the ramada. So light-headed, Slocum could hardly keep his eyes open.

Next thing strong hands carried him out in the bloody sunset.

"My bedroll," he managed to say when they put him an army stretcher between two large mules.

"Where?"

"In the pile."

A woman returned with two of them. He took his own and thanked her. Clutching the roll, a small smile crossed his lips as Posey cussed out a mule. His eyelids shut down.

26

"Where did he go?" Slocum asked, standing on the front porch with crutches under his armpits.

"No good idea. Maybe back to Fronteras." The Apache sat his paint horse and shook his head warily.

"Hernandez got away again?" Jean Myers asked from behind him in the doorway.

"Yes, he's been on the run since the scouts raided his camp. They think he's at Ignacio now." Slocum turned back to Caychem. "I can't ride with you for a few more days."

"Days? Maybe weeks would be more like it," she scoffed at his thoughts of his riding after the bandit.

Caychem smiled big. "I will go up in the mountains and see my woman. Then when I return if you are better we both can ride down there."

"I'll try to be well."

"Wait, you will need some food," Jean shouted, and he reined up the paint. "You men—Lord, lord, head off across no man's land without any food. I've got some jerky and some cookies." She disappeared inside.

"Better come inside," Slocum said, amused at her concern.

The scout bounded off his horse and came up the path to the porch. "You may stay here long time."

"Can't—" He shook his head. He'd spent all morning carving heads on stick horses for the two small ones. Be hard to leave this place, but the word would get out where he was at. In a another few weeks, well or not, he'd have to be on the run again. Be hard to leave her featherbed too for sleeping alone in his old bedroll.

Amantha Grant appreciated all the money he had returned to

her. She hired Carmen to work for her as a trainee under Mrs. Daggett. The five hundred he took out of the belts before returning the rest, he gave privately to Carmen and made her smile.

"Ah, hombre, I owe you much for this." She waved the stack of bills, looking impressed by the amount.

"I owe you my life, pretty woman. That is small pay for what you did for me."

"I would save you again for less." Then she laughed and hugged him tight.

One of Amantha's new hands had driven him round-trip in the buckboard back to Jean Myers. They arrived back after dark and she lit a lamp for him to see by. The cowboy slept in the barn and left after breakfast the next day.

Finished with lunch, Caychem headed for the mountains with a poke full of food. Slocum took a siesta and rose feeling still sore and weak. How would he ever shake the business? Several of the "widows" told him that heatstroke could permanently leave someone that worn-out all the time. He hoped not as he went to sit on the edge of the porch.

Jean was rocking and sewing in her lap.

"You're up again?"

"Barely," he managed, taking his place.

"Maybe I'm killing you at night?" she hissed.

"Good way to die," he said and squeezed her foot.

"I know you have to leave—sooner or later. But the later will suit me fine." The roll of her rocker going back and forth on the board floor made a thumping sound.

"Me too. But you know the story."

"Ain't one dang thing we can do about it either."

"Right."

"There's someone coming from Tombstone."

"Might be the man the church president's sending you."

The rocker paused, she made a dark peeved look at him. "I told that bishop not to be sending me no man. I'd get me a rustler first."

"It's Virgil Earp."

"What does he want?"

"Nothing. Maybe just talk."

"Howdy," Virgil offered, and Slocum waved him off his horse.

"Get up here and met Jean Myers, Virg."

He removed his black hat and smiled coming up the walk. "They said I'd find you here. My pleasure ma'am."

"Nice to meet you. I'll put some coffee on and you men can talk." She set down her sewing and went inside.

"Thought she was a Mormon?"

"She is. Don't drink herself. But makes a fair pot of it."

"Pretty lady. Reason I'm up here, I've got word the Abbott Brothers wired Behan to arrest you and they were coming to take you back."

"Pritchard would like that, wouldn't he? He enjoyed himself the last time arresting me. Besides, Grant paid him the reward on me, they say."

"Why I rode up here."

"How much do I owe you?"

Virg shook his head to dismiss any obligation. "Can't stand Behan, Pritchard, or them overbearing Kansas bastards either."

"Guess I better pack my bags—"

"Not 'till you two drink this pot of coffee," Jean said. "Come in, Marshal."

"The Abbott Brothers are coming, and they want Behan to arrest me."

"You helped Behan get that one outlaw." She looked disgusted over the matter.

"Memories are short in some places."

"Especially when there's money in the deal," Virg added.

She served them coffee and cookies. "Guess you'll slip over the border then?"

"I better."

"What if I take you in my buckboard to John Slaughter's?" she asked.

"What about the kids?"

"Oh, one of the sisters will watch them for that short a period."

"Take two days one way. But I'd worry about you getting back safely."

"Quit worrying, I'd take my old scatter-gun and run anyone of them old border trash off." She took a place at the table.

"She's got a good idea. You don't look strong enough to make that ride on horseback."

"I guess I could always step over the border down there if Pritchard came out to John's."

Virg agreed.

So they loaded the crew in the buckboard and went by Margie Langdon's. She sent her boy Mark over to watch Jean's place and took the children down, hugging each one. The oldest boy Horace wasn't too happy with her fussing over him, but promised his mom to help her watch the little ones.

They made Paul Sutter's ranch in the Mule Shoes by nightfall. The rancher was impressed with the attractive Jean. In fact, the long ride so tired Slocum that he went to sleep shortly after they arrived there, and the two put up her horses.

Dawn cracked the sky and they were hitched and rolling.

"Mr. Sutter's a nice man," she said, holding the horses back going downhill.

"Reckon he'll be by to see you?"

Not looking at him, she wet her lips and looked embarrassed. "He's meeting me tomorrow and guiding me back to his place."

"That's wonderful. All I know about him is good. We've been friends for years."

"Then you aren't angry?"

"About him meeting you tomorrow?"

"Yes."

"I think he'd make a helluva match for you."

She glanced over and smiled. "He might do that then."

When they reached the ranch, John was gone. Buffie took Jean under her wing. They fed Slocum and put him to bed. He didn't recall a thing until the next morning, and he walked Jean to the buckboard in the early light.

"Be careful, big man."

"You too."

"I'll be fine. You ain't mad about Paul?"

"No and he won't have to run."

"Dammit, Slocum, I have to go or I'll cry." He hugged her and kissed her, then helped her up on the seat as she fought bawling. Standing in the cool dawn, he watched her disappear in a cloud of dust. He hugged his arms. He'd damn sure miss that girl.

"Mr. Slocum?"

He turned to the black man, John T. "What's happening?"

"The boss lady say take you down to a Mexican widow lady named Castille and set you up to rest in ole Mexico."

"Anyone comes looking for me?"

John T. laughed aloud. "I tells 'em you done flew the coop."

Juanita Castille was in her forties. Short, petite, and very dark-eyed. She acted as if she expected him and showed him to a hammock in her small courtyard. John T. shook his hand in both of his large calloused paws, then went back to the ranch, not wanting to leave the Mrs. alone for long.

Slocum woke from his nap and she was sitting nearby observing him.

"How long have you been sick?"

He threw his legs over the edge and mopped his face in his hands. "Forever. No, a couple of weeks. Guess I had a heatstroke they say."

"Are you afraid of my medicine?"

"You a doctor?"

She shook her head. "No, I am a *bruja*."

"Cure me and I will be grateful." Witch or whatever, he'd be overwhelmed to have his old strength back.

"You must be hungry?"

"Yes, I'm hungry."

"Good, you must eat many oranges and lemons. They will cure you."

"Many?"

"Many."

"I'm your patient."

"You will soon be well."

So he began Juanita's diet of melons, citrus, and some peaches she located for him.

Slaughter rode down and visited. He drank whiskey, Slocum took lemonade. But he could feel himself growing stronger. John had no word on Hernandez, except the federales wanted him for attempting to rob the Reyes shipment of gold ore, so the noose tightened on the bandit.

The moon was full when Slocum slipped out the French door and stood in the courtyard. What remained of the day's heat was fast expiring; he took a seat in a willow chair. Leaned back, he was enjoying the night insects' sizzle.

Must be recovering, he finally had enough sleep. Then he heard a horse cough like he had a hay seed in his throat. Someone was out there. He slipped into Juanita's dark bedroom. His hand over her mouth he bent over to whisper, "We have company."

Her eyes flew open and she quickly nodded that she understood. From the bedstead side chest she drew out a pistol.

"It is loaded," she assured him, handing the weapon to him.

Quickly, she concealed her nakedness with a robe and tied it on the move. The pistol in his waistband, he herded her to the back of the small house. "Stay here and stay down."

"Oh—"

"Listen, you stay here and do as I say."

"All right, but be careful."

He heard the French doors open and hurried to be in the hallway when they came inside. The gritty sounds of their soles on the floor told him there was more than one person in her bedroom.

"The bed's still warm," someone said in Spanish.

"Hush." The curt familiar voice cut the stillness. Hernandez was there.

Slocum eased along the wall in the pitch-black hallway. The oily smelling Colt close to his face, he eased closer to the doorway.

Then something moved though the frame and he shot. The pistol at his side, he blasted it again. Then he stepped over the downed one and into her room. His ears ringing from the percussion, he rushed in the bedroom in time to see the heels of the other outlaw fleeing the scene.

Outside in the courtyard, he rushed for the gate. The outline of the intruder on his horse made an easy target. The .44 roared in his hand and the rider flew off the side of his skittish horse. Slocum rushed over and raised him up with a fistful of his shirt and shoved the pistol muzzle in his face.

"Who's inside?"

"Hernandez."

"Who in the hell are you?"

"Benito—" The man held his hands up. "I only work for him, senor."

Slocum disarmed and headed him for the courtyard. When he rounded the corner, she stood in her French doors with a lamp.

"This one in here is dead, I think."

"He won't be missed. This one may need some patching."

She crossed herself. "I will try to save him."

"Take that shirt off so she can look at you," he ordered. "Try something, I'll shoot you."

Slocum went to see about the dead man. Slocum had few concerns over Hernandez's fetal-shaped body crumbled in the corner. One more bandit was dead.

"How much is the reward worth on that one?" she asked her patient, bandaging the man's side.

"A hundred pesos."

"Good, you are rich, my friend," she said to Slocum.

"No, you are. I'm riding on in the morning. You've healed me."

"Good," she said and smiled. "We better tie him up then. I have some more of my treatment to use on you before you leave here." Then she chuckled aloud.

It was finally over. Slocum hugged her shoulder and they both laughed.

Watch for

SLOCUM AND THE VANISHED

321st novel in the exciting SLOCUM series
from Jove

Coming in November!

JAKE LOGAN
TODAY'S HOTTEST ACTION WESTERN!